THROUGH THE
EYE OF THE NEEDLE

AMS PRESS
NEW YORK

THROUGH THE
EYE OF THE NEEDLE

A Romance

WITH AN INTRODUCTION

BY
W. D. HOWELLS

HARPER & BROTHERS PUBLISHERS

NEW YORK AND LONDON

1907

Library of Congress Cataloging in Publication Data

Howells, William Dean, 1837-1920.
    Through the eye of the needle.

       Reprint of the 1907 ed. published by Harper, New
York.
    I. Title.
PZ3.H84Thy 1977   [PS2025]   813'.4   74-5475
ISBN 0-404-11548-9

Reprinted by arrangement with Harper & Row, Publishers,
New York, from an original in the collections of the
University of Montana Library

From the edition of 1907, New York
First AMS edition published in 1977
Manufactured in the United States of America

AMS PRESS INC.
NEW YORK, N.Y.

THROUGH THE EYE OF THE NEEDLE

INTRODUCTION

ARISTIDES HOMOS, an Emissary of the Altrurian Commonwealth, visited the United States during the summer of 1893 and the fall and winter following. For some weeks or months he was the guest of a well-known man of letters at a hotel in one of our mountain resorts; in the early autumn he spent several days at the great Columbian Exhibition in Chicago; and later he came to New York, where he remained until he sailed, rather suddenly, for Altruria, taking the circuitous route by which he came. He seems to have written pretty constantly throughout his sojourn with us to an intimate friend in his own country, giving freely his impressions of our civilization. His letters from New York appear to have been especially full, and, in offering the present synopsis of these to the American reader, it will not be impertinent to note certain peculiarities of the Altrurian attitude which the temperament of the writer has somewhat modified. He is entangled in his social sophistries regarding all the competitive civilizations; he cannot apparently do full justice to the superior heroism of charity and self-sacrifice as practised in countries where people live *upon* each other as the Americans do, instead of *for* each other as the Altrurians do; but he has some glimmerings of the beauty of our living, and he has undoubtedly the wish to be fair to our ideals. He is unable to value our devotion to the spirit of Christianity amid

v

the practices which seem to deny it; but he evidently wishes to recognize the possibility of such a thing. He at least accords us the virtues of our defects, and, among the many visitors who have censured us, he has not seen us with his censures prepared to fit the instances; in fact, the very reverse has been his method.

Many of the instances which he fits with his censures are such as he could no longer note, if he came among us again. That habit of celebrating the munificence of the charitable rich, on which he spends his sarcasm, has fallen from us through the mere superabundance of occasion. Our rich people give so continuously for all manner of good objects that it would be impossible for our press, however vigilant, to note the successive benefactions, and millions are now daily bestowed upon needy educational institutions, of which no mention whatever is made in the newspapers. If a millionaire is now and then surprised in a good action by a reporter of uncommon diligence, he is able by an appeal to their common humanity to prevail with the witness to spare him the revolting publicity which it must be confessed would once have followed his discovery; the right hand which is full to overflowing is now as skilled as the empty right hand in keeping the left hand ignorant of its doings. This has happened through the general decay of snobbishness among us, perhaps. It is certain that there is no longer the passion for a knowledge of the rich and the smart, which made us ridiculous to Mr. Homos. Ten or twelve years ago, our newspapers abounded in intelligence of the coming and going of social leaders, of their dinners and lunches and teas, of their receptions and balls, and the guests who were bidden to them. But this sort of unwholesome and exciting gossip, which was formerly devoured by their readers with inappeasable voracity, is no longer supplied, simply because the taste for it has wholly passed away.

Much the same might be said of the social hospitalities which raised our visitor's surprise. For example, many people are now asked to dinner who really need a dinner, and not merely those who revolt from the notion of dinner with loathing, and go to it with abhorrence. At the tables of our highest social leaders one now meets on a perfect equality persons of interesting minds and uncommon gifts who would once have been excluded because they were hungry, or were not in the hostess's set, or had not a new gown or a dress-suit. This contributes greatly to the pleasure of the time, and promotes the increasing kindliness between the rich and poor for which our status is above all things notable.

The accusation which our critic brings that the American spirit has been almost Europeanized away, in its social forms, would be less grounded in the observance of a later visitor. The customs of good society must be the same everywhere in some measure, but the student of the competitive world would now find European hospitality Americanized, rather than American hospitality Europeanized. The careful research which has been made into our social origins has resulted in bringing back many of the aboriginal usages; and, with the return of the old American spirit of fraternity, many of the earlier dishes as well as amenities have been restored. A Thanksgiving dinner in the year 1906 would have been found more like a Thanksgiving dinner in 1806 than the dinner to which Mr. Homos was asked in 1893, and which he has studied so interestingly, though not quite without some faults of taste and discretion. The prodigious change for the better in some material aspects of our status which

has taken place in the last twelve years could nowhere be so well noted as in the picture he gives us
of the housing of our people in 1893. His study
of the evolution of the apartment - house from the
old flat - house, and the still older single dwelling, is
very curious, and, upon the whole, not incorrect.
But neither of these last differed so much from the
first as the apartment - house now differs from the
apartment-house of his day. There are now no dark
rooms opening on airless pits for the family, or black
closets and dismal basements for the servants. Every
room has abundant light and perfect ventilation, and
as nearly a southern exposure as possible. The appointments of the houses are no longer in the spirit
of profuse and vulgar luxury which it must be allowed
once characterized them. They are simply but taste-
fully finished, they are absolutely fireproof, and, with
their less expensive decoration, the rents have been
so far lowered that in any good position a quarter of
nine or ten rooms, with as many baths, can be had for
from three thousand to fifteen thousand dollars. This
fact alone must attract to our metropolis the best of
our population, the bone and sinew which have no
longer any use for themselves where they have been
expended in rearing colossal fortunes, and now demand
a metropolitan repose.

The apartments are much better fitted for a family
of generous size than those which Mr. Homos observed.
Children, who were once almost unheard of, and quite
unheard, in apartment-houses, increasingly abound under favor of the gospel of race preservation. The
elevators are full of them, and in the grassy courts
round which the houses are built, the little ones play
all day long, or paddle in the fountains, warmed with
steam-pipes in the winter, and cooled to an agreeable

temperature in a summer which has almost lost its terrors for the stay-at-home New-Yorker. Each child has his or her little plot of ground in the roof-garden, where they are taught the once wellnigh forgotten art of agriculture.

The improvement of the tenement-house has gone hand in hand with that of the apartment-house. As nearly as the rate of interest on the landlord's investment will allow, the housing of the poor approaches in comfort that of the rich. Their children are still more numerous, and the playgrounds supplied them in every open space and on every pier are visited constantly by the better-to-do children, who exchange with them lessons of form and fashion for the scarcely less valuable instruction in practical life which the poorer little ones are able to give. The rents in the tenement-houses are reduced even more notably than those in the apartment-houses, so that now, with the constant increase in wages, the tenants are able to pay their rents promptly. The evictions once so common are very rare; it is doubtful whether a nightly or daily walk in the poorer quarters of the town would develop, in the coldest weather, half a dozen cases of families set out on the sidewalk with their household goods about them.

The Altrurian Emissary visited this country when it was on the verge of the period of great economic depression extending from 1894 to 1898, but, after the Spanish War, Providence marked the divine approval of our victory in that contest by renewing in unexampled measure the prosperity of the Republic. With the downfall of the trusts, and the release of our industrial and commercial forces to unrestricted activity, the condition of every form of labor has been immeasurably improved, and it is now united with capital in bonds

of the closest affection. But in no phase has its fate
been so brightened as in that of domestic service. This
has occurred not merely through the rise of wages, but
through a greater knowledge between the employing
and employed. When, a few years since, it became
practically impossible for mothers of families to get
help from the intelligence - offices, and ladies were
obliged through lack of cooks and chambermaids to do
the work of the kitchen and the chamber and parlor,
they learned to realize what such work was, how poorly
paid, how badly lodged, how meanly fed. From this
practical knowledge it was impossible for them to retreat to their old supremacy and indifference as mistresses. The servant problem was solved, once for all,
by humanity, and it is doubtful whether, if Mr. Homos
returned to us now, he would give offence by preaching
the example of the Altrurian ladies, or would be shocked by the contempt and ignorance of American women
where other women who did their household drudgery
were concerned.

As women from having no help have learned how
to use their helpers, certain other hardships have been
the means of good. The flattened wheel of the trolley,
banging the track day and night, and tormenting the
waking and sleeping ear, was, oddly enough, the inspiration of reforms which have made our city the quietest
in the world. The trolleys now pass unheard; the
elevated train glides by overhead with only a modu-
lated murmur; the subway is a retreat fit for medita-
tion and prayer, where the passenger can possess his
soul in a peace to be found nowhere else; the auto-
mobile, which was unknown in the day of the Altrurian Emissary, whirs softly through the most crowded
thoroughfare, far below the speed limit, with a sigh
of gentle satisfaction in its own harmlessness, and,

" like the sweet South, taking and giving odor." The
streets that he saw so filthy and unkempt in 1893 are
now at least as clean as they are quiet. Asphalt has
universally replaced the cobble - stones and Belgian
blocks of his day, and, though it is everywhere full of
holes, it is still asphalt, and may some time be put in
repair.

There is a note of exaggeration in his characteriza-
tion of our men which the reader must regret. They are
not now the intellectual inferior of our women, or at
least not so much the inferiors. Since his day they have
made a vast advance in the knowledge and love of lit-
erature. With the multitude of our periodicals, and the
swarm of our fictions selling from a hundred thousand
to half a million each, even our business-men cannot
wholly escape culture, and they have become more and
more cultured, so that now you frequently hear them
asking what this or that book is all about. With the
mention of them, the reader will naturally recur to the
work of their useful and devoted lives—the accumulation of money. It is this accumulation, this heaping-
up of riches, which the Altrurian Emissary accuses in
the love-story closing his study of our conditions, but
which he might not now so totally condemn.

As we have intimated, he has more than once guarded against a rash conclusion, to which the logical habit
of the Altrurian mind might have betrayed him. If
he could revisit us we are sure that he would have still
greater reason to congratulate himself on his forbear-
ance, and would doubtless profit by the lesson which
events must teach all but the most hopeless doctrinaires.
The evil of even a small war (and soldiers themselves
do not deny that wars, large or small, are evil) has,
as we have noted, been overruled for good in the sort
of Golden Age, or Age on a Gold Basis, which we have

long been enjoying. If our good-fortune should be continued to us in reward of our public and private virtue, the fact would suggest to so candid an observer that in economics, as in other things, the rule proves the exception, and that as good times have hitherto always been succeeded by bad times, it stands to reason that our present period of prosperity will never be followed by a period of adversity.

It would seem from the story continued by another hand in the second part of this work, that Altruria itself is not absolutely logical in its events, which are subject to some of the anomalies governing in our own affairs. A people living in conditions which some of our dreamers would consider ideal, are forced to discourage foreign emigration, against their rule of universal hospitality, and in at least one notable instance are obliged to protect themselves against what they believe an evil example by using compulsion with the wrongdoers, though the theory of their life is entirely opposed to anything of the kind. Perhaps, however, we are not to trust to this other hand at all times, since it is a woman's hand, and is not to be credited with the firm and unerring touch of a man's. The story, as she completes it, is the story of the Altrurian's love for an American woman, and will be primarily interesting for that reason. Like the Altrurian's narrative, it is here compiled from a succession of letters, which in her case were written to a friend in America, as his were written to a friend in Altruria. But it can by no means have the sociological value which the record of his observations among ourselves will have for the thoughtful reader. It is at best the record of desultory and imperfect glimpses of a civilization fundamentally alien to her own, such as would attract an enthusiastic nature, but would leave it finally in a sort of misgiving as to the reality of the things seen and heard. Some such misgiving attended the inquiries of those who met the Altrurian during his sojourn with us, but it is a pity that a more absolute conclusion should not have been the effect of this lively lady's knowledge of the ideal country of her adoption. It is, however, an interesting psychological result, and it continues the tradition of all the observers of ideal conditions from Sir Thomas More down to William Morris. Either we have no terms for conditions so unlike our own that they cannot be reported to us with absolute intelligence, or else there is in every experience of them an essential vagueness and uncertainty.

PART FIRST

THROUGH THE EYE OF THE NEEDLE

I

IF I spoke with Altrurian breadth of the way New-Yorkers live, my dear Cyril, I should begin by saying that the New-Yorkers did not live at all. But outside of our happy country one learns to distinguish, and to allow that there are several degrees of living, all indeed hateful to us, if we knew them, and yet none without some saving grace in it. You would say that in conditions where men were embattled against one another by the greed and the envy and the ambition which these conditions perpetually appeal to here, there could be no grace in life; but we must remember that men have always been better than their conditions, and that otherwise they would have remained savages without the instinct or the wish to advance. Indeed, our own state is testimony of a potential civility in all states, which we must keep in mind when we judge the peoples of the plutocratic world, and especially the American people, who are above all others the devotees and exemplars of the plutocratic ideal, without limitation by any aristocracy, theocracy, or monarchy. They are purely commercial, and the thing that cannot be bought and sold has logically no place in their life. But life is not logical outside of Altruria; we are the only people in the world, my dear Cyril, who are privileged to live reasonably; and again I say we must

3

put by our own criterions if we wish to understand the Americans, or to recognize that measure of loveliness which their warped and stunted and perverted lives certainly show, in spite of theory and in spite of conscience, even. I can make this clear to you, I think, by a single instance, say that of the American who sees a case of distress, and longs to relieve it. If he is rich, he can give relief with a good conscience, except for the harm that may come to his beneficiary from being helped; but if he is not rich, or not finally rich, and especially if he has a family dependent upon him, he cannot give in anything like the measure Christ bade us give without wronging those dear to him, immediately or remotely. That is to say, in conditions which oblige every man to look out for himself, a man cannot be a Christian without remorse; he cannot do a generous action without self-reproach; he cannot be nobly unselfish without the fear of being a fool. You would think that this predicament must deprave, and so without doubt it does; and yet it is not wholly depraving. It often has its effect in character of a rare and pathetic sublimity; and many Americans take all the cruel risks of doing good, reckless of the evil that may befall them, and defiant of the upbraidings of their own hearts. This is something that we Altrurians can scarcely understand: it is like the munificence of a savage who has killed a deer and shares it with his starving tribesmen, forgetful of the hungering little ones who wait his return from the chase with food; for life in plutocratic countries is still a chase, and the game is wary and sparse, as the terrible average of failures witnesses.

Of course, I do not mean that Americans may not give at all without sensible risk, or that giving among them is always followed by a logical regret; but, as I said, life with them is in no wise logical. They even applaud one another for their charities, which they measure by the amount given, rather than by the love that goes with the giving. The widow's mite has little credit with them, but the rich man's million has an acclaim that reverberates through their newspapers long after his gift is made. It is only the poor in America who do charity as we do, by giving help where it is needed; the Americans are mostly too busy, if they are at all prosperous, to give anything but money; and the more money they give, the more charitable they esteem themselves. From time to time some man with twenty or thirty millions gives one of them away, usually to a public institution of some sort, where it will have no effect with the people who are underpaid for their work or cannot get work; and then his deed is famed throughout the continent as a thing really beyond praise. Yet any one who thinks about it must know that he never earned the millions he kept, or the millions he gave, but somehow made them from the labor of others; that, with all the wealth left him, he cannot miss the fortune he lavishes, any more than if the check which conveyed it were a withered leaf, and not in any wise so much as an ordinary working-man might feel the bestowal of a postage-stamp.

But in this study of the plutocratic mind, always so fascinating to me, I am getting altogether away from what I meant to tell you. I meant to tell you not how Americans live in the spirit, illogically, blindly, and blunderingly, but how they live in the body, and more especially how they house themselves in this city of New York. A great many of them do not house themselves at all, but that is a class which we cannot now consider, and I will speak only of those who have some sort of a roof over their heads.

5

II

FORMERLY the New-Yorker lived in one of three different ways: in private houses, or boarding-houses, or hotels; there were few restaurants or public tables outside of the hotels, and those who had lodgings and took their meals at eating - houses were but a small proportion of the whole number. The old classification still holds in a measure, but within the last thirty years, or ever since the Civil War, when the enormous commercial expansion of the country began, several different ways of living have been opened. The first and most noticeable of these is housekeeping in flats, or apartments of three or four rooms or more, on the same floor, as in all the countries of Europe except England; though the flat is now making itself known in London, too. Before the war, the New-Yorker who kept house did so in a separate house, three or four stories in height, with a street door of its own. Its pattern within was fixed by long usage, and seldom varied; without, it was of brown - stone before, and brick behind, with an open space there for drying clothes, which was sometimes gardened or planted with trees and vines. The rear of the city blocks which these houses formed was more attractive than the front, as you may still see in the vast succession of monotonous cross-streets not yet invaded by poverty or business; and often the perspective of these rears is picturesque and pleasing. But with the sudden growth of the population when peace came, and through the

6

acquaintance the hordes of American tourists had made with European fashions of living, it became easy, or at least simple, to divide the floors of many of these private dwellings into apartments, each with its own kitchen and all the apparatus of housekeeping. The apartments then had the street entrance and the stairways in common, and they had in common the cellar and the furnace for heating; they had in common the disadvantage of being badly aired and badly lighted. They were dark, cramped, and uncomfortable, but they were cheaper than separate houses, and they were more homelike than boarding - houses or hotels. Large numbers of them still remain in use, and when people began to live in flats, in conformity with the law of evolution, many buildings were put up and subdivided into apartments in imitation of the old dwellings which had been changed.

But the apartment as the New-Yorkers now mostly have it, was at the same time evolving from another direction. The poorer class of New York work-people had for a long period before the war lived, as they still live, in vast edifices, once thought prodigiously tall, which were called tenement-houses. In these a family of five or ten persons is commonly packed in two or three rooms, and even in one room, where they eat and sleep, without the amenities and often without the decencies of life, and of course without light and air. The buildings in case of fire are death-traps; but the law obliges the owners to provide some apparent means of escape, which they do in the form of iron balconies and ladders, giving that festive air to their façades which I have already noted. The bare and dirty entries and staircases are really ramifications of the filthy streets without, and each tenement opens upon a landing as if it opened upon a public thoroughfare. The

7

rents extorted from the inmates is sometimes a hundred per cent., and is nearly always cruelly out of proportion to the value of the houses, not to speak of the wretched shelter afforded; and when the rent is not paid the family in arrears is set with all its poor household gear upon the sidewalk, in a pitiless indifference to the season and the weather, which you could not realize without seeing it, and which is incredible even of plutocratic nature. Of course, landlordism, which you have read so much of, is at its worst in the case of the tenement-houses. But you must understand that comparatively few people in New York own the roofs that shelter them. By far the greater number live, however they live, in houses owned by others, by a class who prosper and grow rich, or richer, simply by owning the roofs over other men's heads. The landlords have, of course, no human relation with their tenants, and really no business relations, for all the affairs between them are transacted by agents. Some have the reputation of being better than others; but they all live, or expect to live, without work, on their rents. They are very much respected for it; the rents are considered a just return from the money invested. You must try to conceive of this as an actual fact, and not merely as a statistical statement. I know it will not be easy for you; it is not easy for me, though I have it constantly before my face.

III

The tenement-house, such as it is, is the original of the apartment - house, which perpetuates some of its most characteristic features on a scale and in material undreamed of in the simple philosophy of the inventor of the tenement-house. The worst of these features is the want of light and air, but as much more space and as many more rooms are conceded as the tenant will pay for. The apartment-house, however, soars to heights that the tenement - house never half reached, and is sometimes ten stories high. It is built fireproof, very often, and is generally equipped with an elevator, which runs night and day, and makes one level of all the floors. The cheaper sort, or those which have departed less from the tenement-house original, have no elevators, but the street door in all is kept shut and locked, and is opened only by the tenant's latch-key or by the janitor having charge of the whole building. In the finer houses there is a page whose sole duty it is to open and shut this door, and who is usually brass-buttoned to one blinding effect of livery with the elevator-boy. Where this page or hall-boy is found, the elevator carries you to the door of any apartment you seek; where he is not found, there is a bell and a speaking-tube in the lower entry, for each apartment, and you ring up the occupant and talk to him as many stories off as he happens to be. But people who can afford to indulge their pride will not live in this sort of apartment-house, and the rents in them are much

9

lower than in the finer sort. The finer sort are vulgarly fine for the most part, with a gaudy splendor of mosaic pavement, marble stairs, frescoed ceilings, painted walls, and cabinet wood-work. But there are many that are fine in a good taste, in the things that are common to the inmates. Their fittings for housekeeping are of all degrees of perfection, and, except for the want of light and air, life in them has a high degree of gross luxury. They are heated throughout with pipes of steam or hot water, and they are sometimes lighted with both gas and electricity, which the inmate uses at will, though of course at his own cost. Outside, they are the despair of architecture, for no style has yet been invented which enables the artist to characterize them with beauty, and wherever they lift their vast bulks they deform the whole neighborhood, throwing the other buildings out of scale, and making it impossible for future edifices to assimilate themselves to the intruder.

There is no end to the apartment-houses for multitude, and there is no street or avenue free from them. Of course, the better sort are to be found on the fashionable avenues and the finer cross-streets, but others follow the course of the horse-car lines on the eastern and western avenues, and the elevated roads on the avenues which these have invaded. In such places they are shops below and apartments above, and I cannot see that the inmates seem at all sensible that they are unfitly housed in them. People are born and married, and live and die in the midst of an uproar so frantic that you would think they would go mad of it; and I believe the physicians really attribute something of the growing prevalence of neurotic disorders to the wear and tear of the nerves from the rush of the trains passing almost momently, and the perpetual jarring of the earth and air from their swift transit. I once spent an evening in one of these apartments, which a friend had taken for a few weeks last spring (you can get them out of season for any length of time), and as the weather had begun to be warm, we had the windows open, and so we had the full effect of the railroad operated under them. My friend had become accustomed to it, but for me it was an affliction which I cannot give you any notion of. The trains seemed to be in the room with us, and I sat as if I had a locomotive in my lap. Their shrieks and groans burst every sentence I began, and if I had not been master of that visible speech which we use so much at home I never should have known what my friend was saying. I cannot tell you how this brutal clamor insulted me, and made the mere exchange of thought a part of the squalid struggle which is the plutocratic conception of life; I came away after a few hours of it, bewildered and bruised, as if I had been beaten upon with hammers.

Some of the apartments on the elevated lines are very good, as such things go; they are certainly costly enough to be good; and they are inhabited by people who can afford to leave them during the hot season when the noise is at its worst; but most of them belong to people who must dwell in them summer and winter, for want of money and leisure to get out of them, and who must suffer incessantly from the noise I could not endure for a few hours. In health it is bad enough, but in sickness it must be horrible beyond all parallel. Imagine a mother with a dying child in such a place; or a wife bending over the pillow of her husband to catch the last faint whisper of farewell, as a train of five or six cars goes roaring by the open window! What horror! what profanation!

11

IV

THE noise is bad everywhere in New York, but in some of the finer apartment-houses on the better streets you are as well out of it as you can be anywhere in the city. I have been a guest in these at different times, and in one of them I am such a frequent guest that I may be said to know its life intimately. In fact, my hostess (women transact society so exclusively in America that you seldom think of your host) in the apartment I mean to speak of, invited me to explore it one night when I dined with her, so that I might, as she said, tell my friends when I got back to Altruria how people lived in America; and I cannot feel that I am violating her hospitality in telling you now. She is that Mrs. Makely whom I met last summer in the mountains, and whom you thought so strange a type from the account of her I gave you, but who is not altogether uncommon here. I confess that, with all her faults, I like her, and I like to go to her house. She is, in fact, a very good woman, perfectly selfish by tradition, as the American women must be, and wildly generous by nature, as they nearly always are; and infinitely superior to her husband in cultivation, as is commonly the case with them. As he knows nothing but business, he thinks it is the only thing worth knowing, and he looks down on the tastes and interests of her more intellectual life with amiable contempt, as something almost comic. She respects business, too, and so she does not despise his ignorance as you would

12

suppose; it is at least the ignorance of a business-man, who must have something in him beyond her ken, or else he would not be able to make money as he does.

With your greater sense of humor, I think you would be amused if you could see his smile of placid self-satisfaction as he listens to our discussion of questions and problems which no more enter his daily life than they enter the daily life of an Eskimo; but I do not find it altogether amusing myself, and I could not well forgive it, if I did not know that he was at heart so simple and good, in spite of his commerciality. But he *is* sweet and kind, as the American men so often are, and he thinks his wife is the delightfulest creature in the world, as the American husband nearly always does. They have several times asked me to dine with them *en famille;* and, as a matter of form, he keeps me a little while with him after dinner, when she has left the table, and smokes his cigar, after wondering why we do not smoke in Altruria; but I can see that he is impatient to get to her in their drawing - room, where we find her reading a book in the crimson light of the canopied lamp, and where he presently falls silent, perfectly happy to be near her. The drawing-room is of a good size itself, and it has a room opening out of it called the library, with a case of books in it, and Mrs. Makely's piano-forte. The place is rather too richly and densely rugged, and there is rather more curtaining and shading of the windows than we should like; but Mrs. Makely is too well up-to-date, as she would say, to have much of the bric-à-brac about which she tells me used to clutter people's houses here. There are some pretty good pictures on the walls, and a few vases and bronzes, and she says she has produced a greater effect of space by quelling the furniture—she means, having few pieces and having them as small as

13

possible. There is a little stand with her afternoon tea - set in one corner, and there is a pretty writing-desk in the library; I remember a sofa and some easy-chairs, but not too many of them. She has a table near one of the windows, with books and papers on it. She tells me that she sees herself that the place is kept just as she wishes it, for she has rather a passion for neatness, and you never can trust servants not to stand the books on their heads or study a vulgar symmetry in the arrangements. She never allows them in there, she says, except when they are at work under her eye; and she never allows anybody there except her guests, and her husband after he has smoked. Of course, her dog must be there; and one evening after her husband fell asleep in the arm-chair near her, the dog fell asleep on the fleece at her feet, and we heard them softly breathing in unison.

She made a pretty little mocking mouth when the sound first became audible, and said that she ought really to have sent Mr. Makely out with the dog, for the dog ought to have the air every day, and she had been kept indoors; but sometimes Mr. Makely came home from business so tired that she hated to send him out, even for the dog's sake, though he was so apt to become dyspeptic. " They won't let you have dogs in some of the apartment-houses, but I tore up the first lease that had that clause in it, and I told Mr. Makely that I would rather live in a house all my days than any flat where my dog wasn't as welcome as I was. Of course, they're rather troublesome."

The Makelys had no children, but it is seldom that the occupants of apartment-houses of a good class have children, though there is no clause in the lease against them. I verified this fact from Mrs. Makely herself, by actual inquiry, for in all the times that I had gone up and down in the elevator to her apartment I had never seen any children. She seemed at first to think I was joking, and not to like it, but when she found that I was in earnest she said that she did not suppose all the families living under that roof had more than four or five children among them. She said that it would be inconvenient; and I could not allege the tenement-houses in the poor quarters of the city, where children seemed to swarm, for it is but too probable that they do not regard convenience in such places, and that neither parents nor children are more comfortable for their presence.

2

V

COMFORT is the American ideal, in a certain way, and comfort is certainly what is studied in such an apartment as the Makelys inhabit. We got to talking about it, and the ease of life in such conditions, and it was then she made me that offer to show me her flat, and let me report to the Altrurians concerning it. She is all impulse, and she asked, How would I like to see it *now?* and when I said I should be delighted, she spoke to her husband, and told him that she was going to show me through the flat. He roused himself promptly, and went before us, at her bidding, to turn up the electrics in the passages and rooms, and then she led the way out through the dining-room.

" This and the parlors count three, and the kitchen here is the fourth room of the eight," she said, and as she spoke she pushed open the door of a small room, blazing with light and dense with the fumes of the dinner and the dish-washing which was now going on in a closet opening out of the kitchen.

She showed me the set range, at one side, and the refrigerator in an alcove, which she said went with the flat, and, " Lena," she said to the cook, " this is the Altrurian gentleman I was telling you about, and I want him to see your kitchen. Can I take him into your room ?"

The cook said, " Oh yes, ma'am," and she gave me a good stare, while Mrs. Makely went to the kitchen window and made me observe that it let in the out-

16

side air, though the court that it opened into was so dark that one had to keep the electrics going in the kitchen night and day. " Of course, it's an expense," she said, as she closed the kitchen door after us. She added, in a low, rapid tone, " You must excuse my introducing the cook. She has read all about you in the papers — you didn't know, I suppose, that there were reporters that day of your delightful talk in the mountains, but I had them—and she was wild, when she heard you were coming, and made me promise to let her have a sight of you somehow. She says she wants to go and live in Altruria, and if you would like to take home a cook, or a servant of any kind, you wouldn't have much trouble. Now here," she ran on, without a moment's pause, while she flung open another door, " is what you won't find in every apartment-house, even very good ones, and that's a back elevator. Sometimes there are only stairs, and they make the poor things climb the whole way up from the basement, when they come in, and all your marketing has to be brought up that way, too; sometimes they send it up on a kind of dumb - waiter, in the cheap places, and you give your orders to the market-men down below through a speaking-tube. But here we have none of that bother, and this elevator is for the kitchen and housekeeping part of the flat. The grocer's and the butcher's man, and anybody who has packages for you, or trunks, or that sort of thing, use it, and, of course, it's for the servants, and they appreciate not having to walk up as much as anybody."

" Oh yes," I said, and she shut the elevator door and opened another a little beyond it.

" This is our guest chamber," she continued, as she ushered me into a very pretty room, charmingly furnished. " It isn't very light by day, for it opens on a

17

court, like the kitchen and the servants' room here," and with that she whipped out of the guest chamber and into another doorway across the corridor. This room was very much narrower, but there were two small beds in it, very neat and clean, with some furnishings that were in keeping, and a good carpet under foot. Mrs. Makely was clearly proud of it, and expected me to applaud it; but I waited for her to speak, which upon the whole she probably liked as well.

" I only keep two servants, because in a flat there isn't really room for more, and I put out the wash and get in cleaning-women when it's needed. I like to use my servants well, because it pays, and I hate to see anybody imposed upon. Some people put in a double-decker, as they call it—a bedstead with two tiers, like the berths on a ship; but I think that's a shame, and I give them two regular beds, even if it does crowd them a little more and the beds have to be rather narrow. This room has outside air, from the court, and, though it's always dark, it's very pleasant, as you see." I did not say that I did not see, and this sufficed Mrs. Makely.

" Now," she said, " I'll show you *our* rooms," and she flew down the corridor towards two doors that stood open side by side and flashed into them before me. Her husband was already in the first she entered, smiling in supreme content with his wife, his belongings, and himself.

" This is a southern exposure, and it has a perfect gush of sun from morning till night. Some of the flats have the kitchen at the end, and that's stupid; you can have a kitchen in any sort of hole, for you can keep on the electrics, and with them the air is perfectly good. As soon as I saw these chambers, and found out that they would let you keep a dog, I told

18

Mr. Makely to sign the lease instantly, and I would see to the rest."

She looked at me, and I praised the room and its dainty tastefulness to her heart's content, so that she said: "Well, it's some satisfaction to show you anything, Mr. Homos, you are so appreciative. I'm sure you'll give a good account of us to the Altrurians. Well, now we'll go back to the pa—drawing-room. This is the end of the story."

"Well," said her husband, with a wink at me, "I thought it was to be continued in our next," and he nodded towards the door that opened from his wife's bower into the room adjoining.

"Why, you poor old fellow!" she shouted. "I forgot all about *your* room," and she dashed into it before us and began to show it off. It was equipped with every bachelor luxury, and with every appliance for health and comfort. "And here," she said, "he can smoke, or anything, as long as he keeps the door shut. Oh, good gracious! I forgot the bath-room," and they both united in showing me this, with its tiled floor and walls and its porcelain tub; and then Mrs. Makely flew up the corridor before us. "Put out the electrics, Dick!" she called back over her shoulder.

VI

WHEN we were again seated in the drawing-room, which she had been so near calling a parlor, she continued to bubble over with delight in herself and her apartment. "Now, isn't it about perfect?" she urged, and I had to own that it was indeed very convenient and very charming; and in the rapture of the moment she invited me to criticise it.

"I see very little to criticise," I said, "from your point of view; but I hope you won't think it indiscreet if I ask a few questions?"

She laughed. "Ask anything, Mr. Homos! I hope I got hardened to your questions in the mountains."

"She said you used to get off some pretty tough ones," said her husband, helpless to take his eyes from her, although he spoke to me.

"It is about your servants," I began.

"Oh, of course! Perfectly characteristic! Go on."

"You told me that they had no natural light either in the kitchen or their bedroom. Do they never see the light of day?"

The lady laughed heartily. "The waitress is in the front of the house several hours every morning at her work, and they both have an afternoon off once a week. Some people only let them go once a fortnight; but I think they are human beings as well as we are, and I let them go *every* week."

"But, except for that afternoon once a week, your cook lives in electric-light perpetually?"

20

"Electric-light is very healthy, and it doesn't heat the air!" the lady triumphed. "I can assure you that she thinks she's very well off; and so she is." I felt a little temper in her voice, and I was silent, until she asked me, rather stiffly, "Is there any *other* inquiry you would like to make?"

"Yes," I said, "but I do not think you would like it."

"Now, I assure you, Mr. Homos, you were never more mistaken in your life. I perfectly delight in your naïveté. I know that the Altrurians don't think as we do about some things, and I don't expect it. What is it you would like to ask?"

"Well, why should you require your servants to go down on a different elevator from yourselves?"

"Why, good gracious!" cried the lady — "aren't they different from us in *every* way? To be sure, they dress up in their ridiculous best when they go out, but you couldn't expect us to let them use the *front* elevator? I don't want to go up and down with my own cook, and I certainly don't with my neighbor's cook!"

"Yes, I suppose you would feel that an infringement of your social dignity. But if you found yourself beside a cook in a horse-car or other public conveyance, you would not feel personally affronted?"

"No, that is a very different thing. That is something we cannot control. But, thank goodness, we *can* control our elevator, and if I were in a house where I had to ride up and down with the servants I would no more stay in it than I would in one where I couldn't keep a dog. I should consider it a perfect outrage. I cannot understand you, Mr. Homos! You are a gentleman, and you must have the traditions of a gentleman, and yet you ask me such a thing as that!"

21

I saw a cast in her husband's eye which I took for a hint not to press the matter, and so I thought I had better say, " It is only that in Altruria we hold serving in peculiar honor."

" Well," said the lady, scornfully, " if you went and got your servants from an intelligence-office, and had to look up their references, you wouldn't hold them in very much honor. I tell you they look out for their interests as sharply as we do for ours, and it's nothing between us but a question of—"

" Business," suggested her husband.

" Yes," she assented, as if this clinched the matter.

" That's what I'm always telling you, Dolly, and yet you *will* try to make them your friends, as soon as you get them into your house. You want them to love you, and you know that sentiment hasn't got anything to do with it."

" Well, I can't help it, Dick. I can't live with a person without trying to like them and wanting them to like me. And then, when the ungrateful things are saucy, or leave me in the lurch as they do half the time, it almost breaks my heart. But I'm thankful to say that in these hard times they won't be apt to leave a good place without a good reason."

" Are there many seeking employment?" I asked this because I thought it was safe ground.

" Well, they just stand around in the office as *thick!*" said the lady. " And the Americans are trying to get places as well as the foreigners. But I won't have Americans. They are too uppish, and they are never half so well trained as the Swedes or the Irish. They still expect to be treated as one of the family. I suppose," she continued, with a lingering ire in her voice, " that in Altruria you do treat them as one of the family ?"

22

"We have no servants, in the American sense," I answered, as inoffensively as I could.

Mrs. Makely irrelevantly returned to the question that had first provoked her indignation. "And I should like to know how much worse it is to have a back elevator for the servants than it is to have the basement door for the servants, as you always do when you live in a separate house?"

"I should think it was no worse," I admitted, and I thought this a good chance to turn the talk from the dangerous channel it had taken. "I wish, Mrs. Makely, you would tell me something about the way people live in separate houses in New York."

She was instantly pacified. "Why, I should be delighted. I only wish my friend Mrs. Bellington Strange was back from Europe; then I could show you a model house. I mean to take you there, as soon as she gets home. She's a kind of Altrurian herself, you know. She was my dearest friend at school, and it almost broke my heart when she married Mr. Strange, so much older, and her inferior in every way. But she's got his money now, and oh, the good she does do with it! I know you'll like each other, Mr. Homos. I do wish Eva was at home!"

I said that I should be very glad to meet an American Altrurian, but that now I wished she would tell me about the normal New York house, and what was its animating principle, beginning with the basement door.

She laughed and said, "Why, it's just like any other house!"

VII

I can never insist enough, my dear Cyril, upon the illogicality of American life. You know what the plutocratic principle is, and what the plutocratic civilization should logically be. But the plutocratic civilization is much better than it should logically be, bad as it is; for the personal equation constantly modifies it, and renders it far less dreadful than you would reasonably expect. That is, the potentialities of goodness implanted in the human heart by the Creator forbid the plutocratic man to be what the plutocratic scheme of life implies. He is often merciful, kindly, and generous, as I have told you already, in spite of conditions absolutely egoistical. You would think that the Americans would be abashed in view of the fact that their morality is often in contravention of their economic principles, but apparently they are not so, and I believe that for the most part they are not aware of the fact. Nevertheless, the fact is there, and you must keep it in mind, if you would conceive of them rightly. You can in no other way account for the contradictions which you will find in my experiences among them; and these are often so bewildering that I have to take myself in hand, from time to time, and ask myself what mad world I have fallen into, and whether, after all, it is not a ridiculous nightmare. I am not sure that, when I return and we talk these things over together, I shall be able to overcome your doubts of my honesty, and I think that when I no longer have them before my eyes I shall begin to doubt my own memory. But for the present I can only set down what I at least seem to see, and trust you to accept it, if you cannot understand it.

Perhaps I can aid you by suggesting that, logically, the Americans should be what the Altrurians are, since their polity embodies our belief that all men are born equal, with the right to life, liberty, and the pursuit of happiness; but that illogically they are what the Europeans are, since they still cling to the economical ideals of Europe, and hold that men are born socially unequal, and deny them the liberty and happiness which can come from equality alone. It is in their public life and civic life that Altruria prevails; it is in their social and domestic life that Europe prevails; and here, I think, is the severest penalty they must pay for excluding women from political affairs; for women are at once the best and the worst Americans: the best because their hearts are the purest, the worst because their heads are the idlest. " Another contradiction!" you will say, and I cannot deny it; for, with all their cultivation, the American women have no real intellectual interests, but only intellectual fads; and while they certainly think a great deal, they reflect little, or not at all. The inventions and improvements which have made their household work easy, the wealth that has released them in such vast numbers from work altogether, has not enlarged them to the sphere of duties which our Altrurian women share with us, but has left them, with their quickened intelligences, the prey of the trivialities which engross the European women, and which have formed the life of the sex hitherto in every country where women have an economical and social freedom without the political freedom that can alone give it dignity and import. They have a great deal of beauty, and they are inconsequently charming; I need not tell you that they are romantic and heroic, or that they would go to the stake for a principle, if they could find one, as willingly as any martyr of the past; but they have not much more perspective than children, and their reading and their talk about reading seem not to have broadened their mental horizons beyond the old sunrise and the old sunset of the kitchen and the parlor.

In fine, the American house as it is, the American household, is what the American woman makes it and wills it to be, whether she wishes it to be so or not; for I often find that the American woman wills things that she in no wise wishes. What the normal New York house is, however, I had great difficulty in getting Mrs. Makely to tell me, for, as she said quite frankly, she could not imagine my not knowing. She asked me if I really wanted her to begin at the beginning, and, when I said that I did, she took a little more time to laugh at the idea, and then she said, " I suppose you mean a brown-stone, four-story house in the middle of a block ?"

" Yes, I think that is what I mean," I said.

" Well," she began, " those high steps that they all have, unless they're English-basement houses, really give them another story, for people used to dine in the front room of their basements. You've noticed the little front yard, about as big as a handkerchief, generally, and the steps leading down to the iron gate, which is kept locked, and the basement door inside the gate ? Well, that's what you might call the back elevator of a house, for it serves the same purpose: the supplies are brought in there, and market-men go in and out, and the ashes, and the swill, and the servants —that you object to so much. We have no alleys in

New York, the blocks are so narrow, north and south; and, of course, we have no back doors; so we have to put the garbage out on the sidewalk — and it's nasty enough, goodness knows. Underneath the sidewalk there are bins where people keep their coal and kindling. You've noticed the gratings in the pavements?"

I said yes, and I was ashamed to own that at first I had thought them some sort of registers for tempering the cold in winter; this would have appeared ridiculous in the last degree to my hostess, for the Americans have as yet no conception of publicly modifying the climate, as we do.

"Back of what used to be the dining-room, and what is now used for a laundry, generally, is the kitchen, with closets between, of course, and then the back yard, which some people make very pleasant with shrubs and vines; the kitchen is usually dark and close, and the girls can only get a breath of fresh air in the yard; I like to see them; but generally it's taken up with clothes-lines, for people in houses nearly all have their washing done at home. Over the kitchen is the dining-room, which takes up the whole of the first floor, with the pantry, and it almost always has a bay-window out of it; of course, that overhangs the kitchen, and darkens it a little more, but it makes the dining-room so pleasant. I tell my husband that I should be almost willing to live in a house again, just on account of the dining-room bay-window. I had it full of flowers in pots, for the southern sun came in; and then the yard was so nice for the dog; you didn't have to take him out for exercise, yourself; he chased the cats there and got plenty of it. I must say that the cats on the back fences were a drawback at night; to be sure, we have them here, too; it's seven stories down, but you

27

do hear 'them, along in the spring. The parlor, or drawing-room, is usually rather long, and runs from the dining - room to the front of the house, though where the house is very deep they have a sort of middle room, or back parlor. Dick, get some paper and draw it. Wouldn't you like to see a plan of the floor?"

I said that I should, and she bade her husband make it like their old house in West Thirty - third Street. We all looked at it together.

" This is the front door," Mrs. Makely explained, " where people come in, and then begins the misery of a house—*stairs!* They mostly go up straight, but sometimes they have them curve a little, and in the new houses the architects have all sorts of little dodges for squaring them and putting landings. Then, on the second floor—draw it, Dick—you have two nice, large chambers, with plenty of light and air, before and behind. I do miss the light and air in a flat, there's no denying it."

" You'll go back to a house yet, Dolly," said her husband.

" Never!" she almost shrieked, and he winked at me, as if it were the best joke in the world. " Never, as long as houses have stairs!"

" Put in an elevator," he suggested.

" Well, that is what Eveleth Strange has, and she lets the servants use it, too," and Mrs. Makely said, with a look at me: " I suppose that would please *you,* Mr. Homos. Well, there's a nice side-room over the front door here, and a bath-room at the rear. Then you have more stairs, and large chambers, and two side-rooms. That makes plenty of chambers for a small family. I used to give two of the third-story rooms to my two girls. I ought really to have made them sleep in one; it seemed such a shame to let the cook have a whole large room to herself; but I had nothing else to do with it, and she did take such comfort in it, poor old thing! You see, the rooms came wrong in our house, for it fronted north, and I had to give the girls, sunny rooms or else give them front rooms, so that it was as broad as it was long. I declare, I was perplexed about it the whole time we lived there, it seemed so perfectly anomalous."

"And what is an English-basement house like?" I ventured to ask, in interruption of the retrospective melancholy she had fallen into.

"Oh, *never* live in an English-basement house, if you value your spine!" cried the lady. "An English-basement house is nothing *but* stairs. In the first place, it's only one room wide, and it's a story higher than the high-stoop house. It's one room forward and one back, the whole way up; and in an English-basement it's always *up,* and *never* down. If I had my way, there wouldn't one stone be left upon another in the English-basements in New York."

I have suffered Mrs. Makely to be nearly as explicit to you as she was to me; for the kind of house she described is of the form ordinarily prevailing in all American cities, and you can form some idea from it how city people live here. I ought perhaps to tell you that such a house is fitted with every housekeeping convenience, and that there is hot and cold water throughout, and gas everywhere. It has fireplaces in all the rooms, where fires are often kept burning for pleasure; but it is really heated from a furnace in the basement, through large pipes carried to the different stories, and opening into them by some such registers as we use. The separate houses sometimes have steam-heating, but not often. They each have their drainage

29

into the sewer of the street, and this is trapped and trapped again, as in the houses of our old plutocratic cities, to keep the poison of the sewer from getting into the houses.

VIII

You will be curious to know something concerning
the cost of living in such a house, and you may be sure
that I did not fail to question Mrs. Makely on this
point. She was at once very volubly communicative;
she told me all she knew, and, as her husband said, a
great deal more.

"Why, of course," she began, "you can spend all
you have in New York, if you like, and people do
spend fortunes every year. But I suppose you mean
the average cost of living in a brown-stone house, in a
good block, that rents for $1800 or $2000 a year, with
a family of three or four children, and two servants.
Well, what should you say, Dick?"

"Ten or twelve thousand a year—fifteen," answered
her husband.

"Yes, fully that," she answered, with an effect of
disappointment in his figures. "We had just ourselves, and we never spent less than seven, and we
didn't dress, and we didn't entertain, either, to speak
of. But you have to live on a certain scale, and generally you live up to your income."

"Quite," said Mr. Makely.

"I don't know what makes it cost so. Provisions
are cheap enough, and they say people live in as good
style for a third less in London. There used to be a
superstition that you could live for less in a flat, and
they always talk to you about the cost of a furnace,
and a man to tend it and keep the snow shovelled off

your sidewalk, but that is all stuff. Five hundred dollars will make up the whole difference, and more. You pay quite as much rent for a decent flat, and then you don't get half the room. No, if it wasn't for the stairs, I wouldn't live in a flat for an instant. But that makes all the difference."

" And the young people," I urged—" those who are just starting in life—how do they manage? Say when the husband has $1500 or $2000 a year?"

" Poor things!" she returned. " I don't know how they manage. They board till they go distracted, or they dry up and blow away; or else the wife has a little money, too, and they take a small flat and ruin themselves. Of course, they want to live nicely and like other people."

" But if they didn't?"

" Why, then they could live delightfully. My husband says he often wishes he was a master-mechanic in New York, with a thousand a year, and a flat for twelve dollars a month; he would have the best time in the world."

Her husband nodded his acquiescence. " Fighting-cock wouldn't be in it," he said. " Trouble is, we all want to do the swell thing."

" But you can't all do it," I ventured, " and, from what I see of the simple, out-of-the-way neighborhoods in my walks, you don't all try."

" Why, no," he said. " Some of us were talking about that the other night at the club, and one of the fellows was saying that he believed there was as much old - fashioned, quiet, almost countrified life in New York, among the great mass of the people, as you'd find in any city in the world. Said you met old codgers that took care of their own furnaces, just as you would in a town of five thousand inhabitants."

"Yes, that's all very well," said his wife; "but they wouldn't be nice people. Nice people want to live nicely. And so they live beyond their means or else they scrimp and suffer. I don't know which is worst."

"But there is no obligation to do either?" I asked.

"Oh yes, there is," she returned. "If you've been born in a certain way, and brought up in a certain way, you can't get out of it. You simply can't. You have got to keep in it till you drop. Or a woman has."

"That means the woman's husband, too," said Mr. Makely, with his wink for me. "Always die together."

In fact, there is the same competition in the social world as in the business world; and it is the ambition of every American to live in some such house as the New York house; and as soon as a village begins to grow into a town, such houses are built. Still, the immensely greater number of the Americans necessarily live so simply and cheaply that such a house would be almost as strange to them as to an Altrurian. But while we should regard its furnishings as vulgar and unwholesome, most Americans would admire and covet its rich rugs or carpets, its papered walls, and thickly curtained windows, and all its foolish ornamentation, and most American women would long to have a house like the ordinary high-stoop New York house, that they might break their backs over its stairs, and become invalids, and have servants about them to harass them and hate them.

Of course, I put it too strongly, for there is often, illogically, a great deal of love between the American women and their domestics, though why there should be any at all I cannot explain, except by reference to that mysterious personal equation which modifies all conditions here. You will have made your reflection that the servants, as they are cruelly called (I have heard them called so in their hearing, and wondered they did not fly tooth and nail at the throat that uttered the insult), form really no part of the house, but are aliens in the household and the family life. In spite of this fact, much kindness grows up between them and the family, and they do not always slight the work that I cannot understand their ever having any heart in. Often they do slight it, and they insist unsparingly upon the scanty privileges which their mistresses seem to think a monstrous invasion of their own rights. The habit of oppression grows upon the oppressor, and you would find tender-hearted women here, gentle friends, devoted wives, loving mothers, who would be willing that their domestics should remain indoors, week in and week out, and, where they are confined in the ridiculous American flat, never see the light of day. In fact, though the Americans do not know it, and would be shocked to be told it, their servants are really slaves, who are none the less slaves because they cannot be beaten, or bought and sold except by the week or month, and for the price which they fix themselves, and themselves receive in the form of wages. They are social outlaws, so far as the society of the family they serve is concerned, and they are restricted in the visits they receive and pay among themselves. They are given the worst rooms in the house, and they are fed with the food that they have prepared, only when it comes cold from the family table; in the wealthier houses, where many of them are kept, they are supplied with a coarser and cheaper victual bought and cooked for them apart from that provided for the family. They are subject, at all hours, to the pleasure or caprice of the master or mistress. Every circumstance of their life is an affront to that just self-respect which even

Americans allow is the right of every human being. With the rich, they are said to be sometimes indolent, dishonest, mendacious, and all that Plato long ago explained that slaves must be; but in the middle-class families they are mostly faithful, diligent, and reliable in a degree that would put to shame most men who hold positions of trust, and would leave many ladies whom they relieve of work without ground for comparison.

IX

AFTER Mrs. Makely had told me about the New York house, we began to talk of the domestic service, and I ventured to hint some of the things that I have so plainly said to you. She frankly consented to my whole view of the matter, for if she wishes to make an effect or gain a point she has a magnanimity that stops at nothing short of self-devotion. " I know it," she said. " You are perfectly right; but here we are, and what are we to do? What do you do in Altruria, I should like to know?"

I said that in Altruria we all worked, and that personal service was honored among us like medical attendance in America; I did not know what other comparison to make; but I said that any one in health would think it as unwholesome and as immoral to let another serve him as to let a doctor physic him. At this Mrs. Makely and her husband laughed so that I found myself unable to go on for some moments, till Mrs. Makely, with a final shriek, shouted to him: " Dick, do stop, or I shall die! Excuse me, Mr. Homos, but you are so deliciously funny, and I know you're just joking. You *won't* mind my laughing? Do go on."

I tried to give her some notion as to how we manage, in our common life, which we have simplified so much beyond anything that this barbarous people dream of; and she grew a little soberer as I went on, and seemed at least to believe that I was not, as her husband said, stuffing them; but she ended, as they always do here, by saying that it might be all very well in Altruria, but it would never do in America, and that it was contrary to human nature to have so many things done in common. " Now, I'll tell you," she said. " After we broke up housekeeping in Thirty-third Street, we stored our furniture—"

" Excuse me," I said. " How—stored ?"

" Oh, I dare say you never store your furniture in Altruria. But here we have hundreds of storage warehouses of all sorts and sizes, packed with furniture that people put into them when they go to Europe, or get sick to death of servants and the whole bother of housekeeping; and that's what we did; and then, as my husband says, we browsed about for a year or two. First, we tried hotelling it, and we took a hotel apartment furnished, and dined at the hotel table, until I certainly thought I should go off, I got so tired of it. Then we hired a suite in one of the family hotels that there are so many of, and got out enough of our things to furnish it, and had our meals in our rooms; they let you do that for the same price, often they are *glad* to have you, for the dining-room is so packed. But everything got to tasting just the same as everything else, and my husband had the dyspepsia so bad he couldn't half attend to business, and I suffered from indigestion myself, cooped up in a few small rooms, that way; and the dog almost died; and finally we gave that up, and took an apartment, and got out our things —the storage cost as much as the rent of a small house —and put them into it, and had a caterer send in the meals as they do in Europe. But it isn't the same here as it is in Europe, and we got so sick of it in a month that I thought I should scream when I saw the same old dishes coming on the table, day after day. We

37

had to keep one servant — excuse me, Mr. Homos: *domestic* — anyway, to look after the table and the parlor and chamber work, and my husband said we might as well be hung for a sheep as a lamb, and so we got in a cook; and, bad as it is, it's twenty million times better than anything else you can do. Servants are a plague, but you have got to have them, and so I have resigned myself to the will of Providence. If they don't like it, neither do I, and so I fancy it's about as broad as it's long." I have found this is a favorite phrase of Mrs. Makely's, and that it seems to give her a great deal of comfort.

" And you don't feel that there's any harm in it?" I ventured to ask.

" Harm in it?" she repeated. " Why, aren't the poor things glad to get the work? What would they do without it?"

" From what I see of your conditions I should be afraid that they would starve," I said.

" Yes, they can't all get places in shops or restaurants, and they have to do something, or starve, as you say," she said; and she seemed to think what I had said was a concession to her position.

" But if it were your own case?" I suggested. " If you had no alternatives but starvation and domestic service, you would think there was harm in it, even although you were glad to take a servant's place?"

I saw her flush, and she answered, haughtily, " You must excuse me if I refuse to imagine myself taking a servant's place, even for the sake of argument."

" And you are quite right," I said. " Your American instinct is too strong to brook even in imagination the indignities which seem daily, hourly, and momently inflicted upon servants in your system."

To my great astonishment she seemed delighted by

this conclusion. " Yes," she said, and she smiled radiantly, " and now you understand how it is that American girls won't go out to service, though the pay is so much better and they are so much better housed and fed—and everything. Besides," she added, with an irrelevance which always amuses her husband, though I should be alarmed by it for her sanity if I did not find it so characteristic of women here, who seem to be mentally characterized by the illogicality of the civilization, " they're not half so good as the foreign servants. They've been brought up in homes of their own, and they're uppish, and they have no idea of anything but third - rate boarding - house cooking, and they're always hoping to get married, so that, really, you have no peace of your life with them."

" And it never seems to you that the whole relation is wrong ?" I asked.

" What relation ?"

" That between maid and mistress, the hirer and the hireling."

" Why, good gracious!" she burst out. " Didn't Christ himself say that the laborer was worthy of his hire ? And how would you get your work done, if you didn't pay for it ?"

" It might be done for you, when you could not do it yourself, from affection."

" From affection!" she returned, with the deepest derision. " Well, I rather think I *shall* have to do it myself if I want it done from affection! But I suppose you think I *ought* to do it myself, as the Altrurian ladies do! I can tell you that in America it would be impossible for a lady to do her own work, and there are no intelligence-offices where you can find girls that want to work for love. It's as broad as it's long."

"It's simply business," her husband said.

They were right, my dear friend, and I was wrong, strange as it must appear to you. The tie of service, which we think as sacred as the tie of blood, can be here only a business relation, and in these conditions service must forever be grudgingly given and grudgingly paid. There is something in it, I do not quite know what, for I can never place myself precisely in an American's place, that degrades the poor creatures who serve, so that they must not only be social outcasts, but must leave such a taint of dishonor on their work that one cannot even do it for one's self without a sense of outraged dignity. You might account for this in Europe, where ages of prescriptive wrong have distorted the relation out of all human wholesomeness and Christian loveliness; but in America, where many, and perhaps most, of those who keep servants and call them so are but a single generation from fathers who earned their bread by the sweat of their brows, and from mothers who nobly served in all household offices, it is in the last degree bewildering. I can only account for it by that bedevilment of the entire American ideal through the retention of the English economy when the English polity was rejected. But at the heart of America there is this ridiculous contradiction, and it must remain there until the whole country is Altrurianized. There is no other hope; but I did not now urge this point, and we turned to talk of other things, related to the matters we had been discussing.

"The men," said Mrs. Makely, "get out of the whole bother very nicely, as long as they are single, and even when they're married they are apt to run off to the club when there's a prolonged upheaval in the kitchen."

"*I* don't, Dolly," suggested her husband.

"No, *you* don't, Dick," she returned, fondly. "But there are not many like you."

He went on, with a wink at me, "I never live at the club, except in summer, when you go away to the mountains."

"Well, you know I can't very well take you with me," she said.

"Oh, I couldn't leave my business, anyway," he said, and he laughed.

X

I HAD noticed the vast and splendid club-houses in the best places in the city, and I had often wondered about their life, which seemed to me a blind groping towards our own, though only upon terms that forbade it to those who most needed it. The clubs here are not like our groups, the free association of sympathetic people, though one is a little more literary, or commercial, or scientific, or political than another; but the entrance to each is more or less jealously guarded; there is an initiation-fee, and there are annual dues, which are usually heavy enough to exclude all but the professional and business classes, though there are, of course, successful artists and authors in them. During the past winter I visited some of the most characteristic, where I dined and supped with the members, or came alone when one of these put me down, for a fortnight or a month.

They are equipped with kitchens and cellars, and their wines and dishes are of the best. Each is, in fact, like a luxurious private house on a large scale; outwardly they are palaces, and inwardly they have every feature and function of a princely residence complete, even to a certain number of guest - chambers, where members may pass the night, or stay indefinitely in some cases, and actually live at the club. The club, however, is known only to the cities and larger towns, in this highly developed form; to the ordinary, simple American of the country, or of the country town of five or ten thousand people, a New York club would be as strange as it would be to any Altrurian.

"Do many of the husbands left behind in the summer live at the club?" I asked.

"All that *have* a club do," he said. "Often there's a very good table d'hôte dinner that you couldn't begin to get for the same price anywhere else; and there are a lot of good fellows there, and you can come pretty near forgetting that you're homeless, or even that you're married."

He laughed, and his wife said: "You ought to be ashamed, Dick; and me worrying about you all the time I'm away, and wondering what the cook gives you here. Yes," she continued, addressing me, "that's the worst thing about the clubs. They make the men so comfortable that they say it's one of the principal obstacles to early marriages. The young men try to get lodgings near them, so that they can take their meals there, and they know they get much better things to eat than they could have in a house of their own at a great deal more expense, and so they simply don't think of getting married. Of course," she said, with that wonderful, unintentional, or at least unconscious, frankness of hers, "I don't blame the clubs altogether. There's no use denying that girls are expensively brought up, and that a young man has to think twice before taking one of them out of the kind of home she's used to and putting her into the kind of home he can give her. If the clubs have killed early marriages, the women have created the clubs."

"Do women go much to them?" I asked, choosing this question as a safe one.

"*Much!*" she screamed. "They don't go at all! They *can't!* They won't *let* us! To be sure, there are some that have rooms where ladies can go with their friends who are members, and have lunch or dinner; but as for seeing the inside of the club-house proper, where these great creatures "—she indicated her husband—" are sitting up, smoking and telling stories, it isn't to be dreamed of."

Her husband laughed. " You wouldn't like the smoking, Dolly."

" Nor the stories, some of them," she retorted.

" Oh, the stories are always first-rate," he said, and he laughed more than before.

" And they never gossip at the clubs, Mr. Homos—never!" she added.

" Well, hardly ever," said her husband, with an intonation that I did not understand. It seemed to be some sort of catch-phrase.

" All I know," said Mrs. Makely, " is that I like to have my husband belong to his club. It's a nice place for him in summer; and very often in winter, when I'm dull, or going out somewhere that he hates, he can go down to his club and smoke a cigar, and come home just about the time I get in, and it's much better than worrying through the evening with a book. He hates books, poor Dick!" She looked fondly at him, as if this were one of the greatest merits in the world. " But I confess I shouldn't like him to be a mere club man, like some of them."

" But how ?" I asked.

" Why, belonging to five or six, or more, even; and spending their whole time at them, when they're not at business."

There was a pause, and Mr. Makely put on an air of modest worth, which he carried off with his usual wink towards me. I said, finally, " And if the ladies are not admitted to the men's clubs, why don't they have clubs of their own ?"

" Oh, they have—several, I believe. But who wants to go and meet a lot of women ? You meet enough of them in society, goodness knows. You hardly meet any one else, especially at afternoon teas. They bore you to death."

Mrs. Makely's nerves seemed to lie in the direction of a prolongation of this subject, and I asked my next question a little away from it. " I wish you would tell me, Mrs. Makely, something about your way of provisioning your household. You said that the grocer's and butcher's man came up to the kitchen with your supplies—"

" Yes, and the milkman and the iceman; the iceman always puts the ice into the refrigerator; it's very convenient, and quite like your own house."

" But you go out and select the things yourself the day before, or in the morning?"

" Oh, not at all! The men come and the cook gives the order; she knows pretty well what we want on the different days, and I never meddle with it from one week's end to the other, unless we have friends. The tradespeople send in their bills at the end of the month, and that's all there is of it." Her husband gave me one of his queer looks, and she went on: " When we were younger, and just beginning housekeeping, I used to go out and order the things myself; I used even to go to the big markets, and half kill myself trying to get things a little cheaper at one place and another, and waste more car-fare and lay up more doctor's bills than it would all come to, ten times over. I used to fret my life out, remembering the prices; but now, thank goodness, that's all over. I don't know any more what beef is a pound than my husband does; if a thing isn't good, I send it straight back, and that puts them on their honor, you know, and they have to give me the

45

best of everything. The bills average about the same, from month to month; a little more if we have company; but if they're too outrageous, I make a fuss with the cook, and she scolds the men, and then it goes better for a while. Still, it's a great bother."

I confess that I did not see what the bother was, but I had not the courage to ask, for I had already conceived a wholesome dread of the mystery of an American lady's nerves. So I merely suggested, " And that is the way that people usually manage ?"

" Why," she said, " I suppose that some old-fashioned people still do their marketing, and people that have to look to their outgoes, and know what every mouthful costs them. But their lives are not worth having. Eveleth Strange does it — or she did do it when she was in the country; I dare say she won't when she gets back—just from a sense of duty, and because she says that a housekeeper ought to know about her expenses. But I ask her who will care whether she knows or not; and as for giving the money to the poor that she saves by spending economically, I tell her that the butchers and the grocers have to live, too, as well as the poor, and so it's as broad as it's long."

XI

I could not make out whether Mr. Makely approved of his wife's philosophy or not; I do not believe he thought much about it. The money probably came easily with him, and he let it go easily, as an American likes to do. There is nothing penurious or sordid about this curious people, so fierce in the pursuit of riches. When these are once gained, they seem to have no value to the man who has won them, and he has generally no object in life but to see his womankind spend them.

This is the season of the famous Thanksgiving, which has now become the national holiday, but has no longer any savor in it of the grim Puritanism it sprang from. It is now appointed by the president and the governors of the several states, in proclamations enjoining a pious gratitude upon the people for their continued prosperity as a nation, and a public acknowledgment of the divine blessings. The blessings are supposed to be of the material sort, grouped in the popular imagination as good times, and it is hard to see what they are when hordes of men and women of every occupation are feeling the pinch of poverty in their different degrees. It is not merely those who have always the wolf at their doors who are now suffering, but those whom the wolf never threatened before; those who amuse as well as those who serve the rich are alike anxious and fearful, where they are not already in actual want; thousands of poor players, as well as hundreds of thousands of poor laborers, are out of employment, and the winter threatens to be one of dire misery. Yet you would not imagine from the smiling face of things, as you would see it in the better parts of this great city, that there was a heavy heart or an empty stomach anywhere below it. In fact, people here are so used to seeing other people in want that it no longer affects them as reality; it is merely dramatic, or hardly so lifelike as that—it is merely histrionic. It is rendered still more spectacular to the imaginations of the fortunate by the melodrama of charity they are invited to take part in by endless appeals, and their fancy is flattered by the notion that they are curing the distress they are only slightly relieving by a gift from their superfluity. The charity, of course, is better than nothing, but it is a fleeting mockery of the trouble, at the best. If it were proposed that the city should subsidize a theatre at which the idle players could get employment in producing good plays at a moderate cost to the people, the notion would not be considered more ridiculous than that of founding municipal works for the different sorts of idle workers; and it would not be thought half so nefarious, for the proposition to give work by the collectivity is supposed to be in contravention of the sacred principle of monopolistic competition so dear to the American economist, and it would be denounced as an approximation to the surrender of the city to anarchism and destruction by dynamite.

But as I have so often said, the American life is in no wise logical, and you will not be surprised, though you may be shocked or amused, to learn that the festival of Thanksgiving is now so generally devoted to witnessing a game of football between the elevens of two great universities that the services at the churches are very scantily attended. The Americans are practical, if they are not logical, and this preference of football to prayer and praise on Thanksgiving-day has gone so far that now a principal church in the city holds its services on Thanksgiving - eve, so that the worshippers may not be tempted to keep away from their favorite game.

There is always a heavy dinner at home after the game, to console the friends of those who have lost and to heighten the joy of the winning side, among the comfortable people. The poor recognize the day largely as a sort of carnival. They go about in masquerade on the eastern avenues, and the children of the foreign races who populate that quarter penetrate the better streets, blowing horns and begging of the passers. They have probably no more sense of its difference from the old carnival of Catholic Europe than from the still older Saturnalia of pagan times. Perhaps you will say that a masquerade is no more pagan than a football game; and I confess that I have a pleasure in that innocent misapprehension of the holiday on the East Side. I am not more censorious of it than I am of the displays of festival cheer at the provision-stores or green-groceries throughout the city at this time. They are almost as numerous on the avenues as the drinking-saloons, and, thanks to them, the wasteful housekeeping is at least convenient in a high degree. The waste is inevitable with the system of separate kitchens, and it is not in provisions alone, but in labor and in time, a hundred cooks doing the work of one; but the Americans have no conception of our co - operative housekeeping, and so the folly goes on.

Meantime the provision - stores add much to their effect of crazy gayety on the avenues. The variety and harmony of colors is very great, and this morn-

49

ing I stood so long admiring the arrangement in one of them that I am afraid I rendered myself a little suspicious to the policeman guarding the liquor-store on the nearest corner; there seems always to be a policeman assigned to this duty. The display was on either side of the provisioner's door, and began, on one hand, with a basal line of pumpkins well out on the sidewalk. Then it was built up with the soft white and cool green of cauliflowers and open boxes of red and white grapes, to the window that flourished in banks of celery and rosy apples. On the other side, gray-green squashes formed the foundation, and the wall was sloped upward with the delicious salads you can find here, the dark red of beets, the yellow of carrots, and the blue of cabbages. The association of colors was very artistic, and even the line of mutton carcases overhead, with each a brace of grouse or half a dozen quail in its embrace, and flanked with long sides of beef at the four ends of the line, was picturesque, though the sight of the carnage at the provision-stores here would always be dreadful to an Altrurian; in the great markets it is intolerable. This sort of business is mostly in the hands of the Germans, who have a good eye for such effects as may be studied in it; but the fruiterers are nearly all Italians, and their stalls are charming. I always like, too, the cheeriness of the chestnut and peanut ovens of the Italians; the pleasant smell and friendly smoke that rise from them suggest a simple and homelike life which there are so many things in this great, weary, heedless city to make one forget.

XII

But I am allowing myself to wander too far from Mrs. Makely and her letter, which reached me only two days before Thanksgiving.

"My dear Mr. Homos,—Will you give me the pleasure of your company at dinner, on Thanksgiving-day, at eight o'clock, very informally. My friend, Mrs. Bellington Strange, has unexpectedly returned from Europe within the week, and I am asking a few friends, whom I can trust to excuse this very short notice, to meet her.

"With Mr. Makely's best regards,
"Yours cordially,
"Dorothea Makely.

"The Sphinx,
November the twenty sixth,
Eighteen hundred and
Ninety-three."

I must tell you that it has been a fad with the ladies here to spell·out their dates, and, though the fashion is waning, Mrs. Makely is a woman who would remain in such an absurdity among the very last. I will let you make your own conclusions concerning this, for though, as an Altrurian, I cannot respect her, I like her so much, and have so often enjoyed her generous hospitality, that I cannot bring myself to criticise her except by the implication of the facts. She is anomalous, but, to our way of thinking, all the Americans I have met are anomalous, and she has the merits that you would not logically attribute to her character. Of course, I cannot feel that her evident regard for me is

51

the least of these, though I like to think that it is founded on more reason than the rest.

I have by this time become far too well versed in the polite insincerities of the plutocratic world to imagine that, because she asked me to come to her dinner very informally, I was not to come in all the state I could put into my dress. You know what the evening dress of men is here, from the costumes in our museum, and you can well believe that I never put on those ridiculous black trousers without a sense of their grotesqueness—that scrap of waistcoat reduced to a mere rim, so as to show the whole white breadth of the starched shirt-bosom, and that coat chopped away till it seems nothing but tails and lapels. It is true that I might go out to dinner in our national costume; in fact, Mrs. Makely has often begged me to wear it, for she says the Chinese wear theirs; but I have not cared to make the sensation which I must if I wore it; my outlandish views of life and my frank study of their customs signalize me quite sufficiently among the Americans.

At the hour named I appeared in Mrs. Makely's drawing-room in all the formality that I knew her invitation, to come very informally, really meant. I found myself the first, as I nearly always do, but I had only time for a word or two with my hostess before the others began to come. She hastily explained that as soon as she knew Mrs. Strange was in New York she had despatched a note telling her that I was still here; and that as she could not get settled in time to dine at home, she must come and take Thanksgiving dinner with her. " She will have to go out with Mr. Makely; but I am going to put you next to her at table, for I want you both to have a good time. But don't you forget that you are going to take *me* out."

I said that I should certainly not forget it, and I showed her the envelope with my name on the outside, and hers on a card inside, which the serving-man at the door had given me in the hall, as the first token that the dinner was to be unceremonious.

She laughed, and said: " I've had the luck to pick up two or three other agreeable people that I know will be glad to meet you. Usually it's such a scratch lot at Thanksgiving, for everybody dines at home that can, and you have to trust to the highways and the byways for your guests, if you give a dinner. But I did want to bring Mrs. Strange and you together, and so I chanced it. Of course, it's a sent-in dinner, as you must have inferred from the man at the door; I've given my servants a holiday, and had Claret's people do the whole thing. It's as broad as it's long, and, as my husband says, you might as well be hung for a sheep as a lamb; and it saves bother. Everybody will know it's sent in, so that nobody will be deceived. There'll be a turkey in it somewhere, and cranberry sauce; I've insisted on that; but it won't be a regular American Thanksgiving dinner, and I'm rather sorry, on your account, for I wanted you to see one, and I meant to have had you here, just with ourselves; but Eveleth Strange's coming back put a new face on things, and so I've gone in for this affair, which isn't at all what you would like. That's the reason I tell you at once it's sent in."

XIII

I AM so often at a loss for the connection in Mrs. Makely's ideas that I am more patient with her incoherent jargon than you will be, I am afraid. It went on to much the effect that I have tried to report until the moment she took the hand of the guest who came next. They arrived, until there were eight of us in all, Mrs. Strange coming last, with excuses for being late. I had somehow figured her as a person rather mystical and recluse in appearance, perhaps on account of her name, and I had imagined her tall and superb. But she was, really, rather small, though not below the woman's average, and she had a face more round than otherwise, with a sort of business-like earnestness, but a very charming smile, and presently, as I saw, an American sense of humor. She had brown hair and gray eyes, and teeth not too regular to be monotonous; her mouth was very sweet, whether she laughed or sat gravely silent. She at once affected me like a person who had been sobered beyond her nature by responsibilities, and had steadily strengthened under the experiences of life. She was dressed with a sort of personal taste, in a rich gown of black lace, which came up to her throat; and she did not subject me to that embarrassment I always feel in the presence of a lady who is much décolletée, when I sit next her or face to face with her: I cannot always look at her without a sense of taking an immodest advantage. Sometimes I find a kind of pathos in this

54

sacrifice of fashion, which affects me as if the poor lady were wearing that sort of gown because she thought she really ought, and then I keep my eyes firmly on hers, or avert them altogether; but there are other cases which have not this appealing quality. Yet in the very worst of the cases it would be a mistake to suppose that there was a display personally meant of the display personally made. Even then it would be found that the gown was worn so because the dressmaker had made it so, and, whether she had made it in this country or in Europe, that she had made it in compliance with a European custom. In fact, all the society customs of the Americans follow some European original, and usually some English original; and it is only fair to say that in this particular custom they do not go to the English extreme.

We did not go out to dinner at Mrs. Makely's by the rules of English precedence, because there are nominally no ranks here, and we could not; but I am sure it will not be long before the Americans will begin playing at precedence just as they now play at the other forms of aristocratic society. For the present, however, there was nothing for us to do but to proceed, when dinner was served, in such order as offered itself, after Mr. Makely gave his arm to Mrs. Strange; though, of course, the white shoulders of the other ladies went gleaming out before the white shoulders of Mrs. Makely shone beside my black ones. I have now become so used to these observances that they no longer affect me as they once did, and as I suppose my account of them must affect you, painfully, comically. But I have always the sense of having a part in amateur theatricals, and I do not see how the Americans can fail to have the same sense, for there is nothing spontaneous in them, and nothing that has grown even dramatically out of their own life.

Often when I admire the perfection of the stage-setting, it is with a vague feeling that I am derelict in not offering it an explicit applause. In fact, this is permitted in some sort and measure, as now when we sat down at Mrs. Makely's exquisite table, and the ladies frankly recognized her touch in it. One of them found a phrase for it at once, and pronounced it a symphony in chrysanthemums; for the color and the character of these flowers played through all the appointments of the table, and rose to a magnificent finale in the vast group in the middle of the board, infinite in their caprices of tint and design. Another lady said that it was a dream, and then Mrs. Makely said, " No, a memory," and confessed that she had studied the effect from her recollection of some tables at a chrysanthemum show held here year before last, which seemed failures because they were so simply and crudely adapted in the china and napery to merely one kind and color of the flower.

" Then," she added, " I wanted to do something very chrysanthemummy, because it seems to me the Thanksgiving flower, and belongs to Thanksgiving quite as much as holly belongs to Christmas."

Everybody applauded her intention, and they hungrily fell to upon the excellent oysters, with her warning that we had better make the most of everything in its turn, for she had conformed her dinner to the brevity of the notice she had given her guests.

XIV

Just what the dinner was I will try to tell you, for
I think that it will interest you to know what people
here think a very simple dinner. That is, people of
any degree of fashion; for the unfashionable Americans, who are innumerably in the majority, have, no
more than the Altrurians, seen such a dinner as Mrs.
Makely's. This sort generally sit down to a single dish
of meat, with two or three vegetables, and they drink
tea or coffee, or water only, with their dinner. Even
when they have company, as they say, the things are
all put on the table at once; and the average of Americans who have seen a dinner served in courses, after
the Russian manner, invariable in the fine world here,
is not greater than those who have seen a serving-man
in livery. Among these the host piles up his guest's
plate with meat and vegetables, and it is passed from
hand to hand till it reaches him; his drink arrives from
the hostess by the same means. One maid serves the
table in a better class, and two maids in a class still
better; it is only when you reach people of very decided
form that you find a man in a black coat behind your
chair; Mrs. Makely, mindful of the informality of the
her dinner in everything, had two men.

I should say the difference between the Altrurians
and the unfashionable Americans, in view of such a
dinner as she gave us, would be that, while it would
seem to us abominable for its extravagance, and revolting in its appeals to appetite, it would seem to most

57

of such Americans altogether admirable and enviable, and would appeal to their ambition to give such a dinner themselves as soon as ever they could.

Well, with our oysters we had a delicate French wine, though I am told that formerly Spanish wines were served. A delicious soup followed the oysters, and then we had fish with sliced cucumbers dressed with oil and vinegar, like a salad; and I suppose you will ask what we could possibly have eaten more. But this was only the beginning, and next there came a course of sweetbreads with green pease. With this the champagne began at once to flow, for Mrs. Makely was nothing if not original, and she had champagne very promptly. One of the gentlemen praised her for it, and said you could not have it too soon, and he had secretly hoped it would have begun with the oysters. Next, we had a remove — a tenderloin of beef, with mushrooms, fresh, and not of the canned sort which it is usually accompanied with. This fact won our hostess more compliments from the gentlemen, which could not have gratified her more if she had dressed and cooked the dish herself. She insisted upon our trying the stewed terrapin, for, if it did come in a little by the neck and shoulders, it was still in place at a Thanksgiving dinner, because it was so American; and the stuffed peppers, which, if they were not American, were at least Mexican, and originated in the kitchen of a sister republic. There were one or two other side-dishes, and, with all, the burgundy began to be poured out.

Mr. Makely said that claret all came now from California, no matter what French château they named it after, but burgundy you could not err in. His guests were now drinking the different wines, and to much the same effect, I should think, as if they had mixed them all in one cup; though I ought to say that several of the ladies took no wine, and kept me in countenance after the first taste I was obliged to take of each, in order to pacify my host.

You must know that all the time there were plates of radishes, olives, celery, and roasted almonds set about that every one ate of without much reference to the courses. The talking and the feasting were at their height, but there was a little flagging of the appetite, perhaps, when it received the stimulus of a water-ice flavored with rum. After eating it I immediately experienced an extraordinary revival of my hunger (I am ashamed to confess that I was gorging myself like the rest), but I quailed inwardly when one of the men-servants set down before Mr. Makely a roast turkey that looked as large as an ostrich. It was received with cries of joy, and one of the gentlemen said, " Ah, Mrs. Makely, I was waiting to see how you would interpolate the turkey, but you never fail. I knew you would get it in somewhere. But where," he added, in a burlesque whisper, behind his hand, " are the—"

" Canvasback duck ?" she asked, and at that moment the servant set before the anxious inquirer a platter of these renowned birds, which you know something of already from the report our emissaries have given of their cult among the Americans.

Every one laughed, and after the gentleman had made a despairing flourish over them with a carving-knife in emulation of Mr. Makely's emblematic attempt upon the turkey, both were taken away and carved at a sideboard. They were then served in slices, the turkey with cranberry sauce, and the ducks with currant jelly; and I noticed that no one took so much of the turkey that he could not suffer himself to be helped also to the duck. I must tell you that there was a salad with the duck, and after that there was an ice-cream, with fruit and all manner of candied fruits, and candies, different kinds of cheese, coffee, and liqueurs to drink after the coffee.

"Well, now," Mrs. Makely proclaimed, in high delight with her triumph, "I must let you imagine the pumpkin - pie. I meant to have it, because it isn't really Thanksgiving without it. But I couldn't, for the life of me, see where it would come in."

XV

THE sally of the hostess made them all laugh, and they began to talk about the genuine American character of the holiday, and what a fine thing it was to have something truly national. They praised Mrs. Makely for thinking of so many American dishes, and the facetious gentleman said that she rendered no greater tribute than was due to the overruling Providence which had so abundantly bestowed them upon the Americans as a people. " You must have been glad, Mrs. Strange," he said to the lady at my side, " to get back to our American oysters. There seems nothing else so potent to bring us home from Europe."

" I'm afraid," she answered, " that I don't care so much for the American oyster as I should. But I am certainly glad to get back."

" In time for the turkey, perhaps ?"

" No, I care no more for the turkey than for the oyster of my native land," said the lady.

" Ah, well, say the canvasback duck, then ? The canvasback duck is no alien. He is as thoroughly American as the turkey, or as any of us."

" No, I should not have missed him, either," persisted the lady.

" What could one have missed," the gentleman said, with a bow to the hostess, " in the dinner Mrs. Makely has given us ? If there had been nothing, I should not have missed it," and when the laugh at his drolling had subsided he asked Mrs. Strange: " Then, if it is not too indiscreet, might I inquire what in the world has lured you again to our shores, if it was not the oyster, nor the turkey, nor yet the canvasback?"

" The American dinner - party," said the lady, with the same burlesque.

" Well," he consented, " I think I understand you. It is different from the English dinner-party in being a festivity rather than a solemnity; though, after all, the American dinner is only a condition of the English dinner. Do you find us much changed, Mrs. Strange?"

" I think we are every year a little more European," said the lady. " One notices it on getting home."

" I supposed we were so European already," returned the gentleman, " that a European landing among us would think he had got back to his starting-point in a sort of vicious circle. I am myself so thoroughly Europeanized in all my feelings and instincts that, do you know, Mrs. Makely, if I may confess it without offence—"

" Oh, by all means!" cried the hostess.

" When that vast bird which we have been praising, that colossal roast turkey, appeared, I felt a shudder go through my delicate substance, such as a refined Englishman might have experienced at the sight, and I said to myself, quite as if I were not one of you, " Good Heavens! now they will begin talking through their noses and eating with their knives. It's what I might have expected!"

It was impossible not to feel that this gentleman was talking at me; if the Americans have a foreign guest, they always talk at him more or less; and I was not surprised when he said, " I think our friend, Mr. Homos, will conceive my fine revolt from the crude period of our existence which the roast turkey marks as distinctly as the *graffiti* of the cave-dweller proclaim his epoch."

" No," I protested, " I am afraid that I have not the documents for the interpretation of your emotion. I hope you will take pity on my ignorance and tell me just what you mean."

The others said they none of them knew, either, and would like to know, and the gentleman began by saying that he had been going over the matter in his mind on his way to dinner, and he had really been trying to lead up to it ever since we sat down. " I've been struck, first of all, by the fact, in our evolution, that we haven't socially evolved from ourselves; we've evolved from the Europeans, from the English. I don't think you'll find a single society rite with us now that had its origin in our peculiar national life, if we have a peculiar national life; I doubt it, sometimes. If you begin with the earliest thing in the day, if you begin with breakfast, as society gives breakfasts, you have an English breakfast, though American people and provisions."

" I must say, I think they're both much nicer," said Mrs. Makely.

" Ah, there I am with you! We borrow the form, but we infuse the spirit. I am talking about the form, though. Then, if you come to the society lunch, which is almost indistinguishable from the society breakfast, you have the English lunch, which is really an under-sized English dinner. The afternoon tea is English again, with its troops of eager females and stray, reluctant males; though I believe there are rather more men at the English teas, owing to the larger leisure class in England. The afternoon tea and the ' at home ' are as nearly alike as the breakfast and the lunch. Then, in the course of time, we arrive at the

s

great society function, the dinner; and what is the dinner with us but the dinner of our mother - country?"

"It is livelier," suggested Mrs. Makely, again.

"Livelier, I grant you, but I am still speaking of the form, and not of the spirit. The evening reception, which is gradually fading away, as a separate rite, with its supper and its dance, we now have as the English have it, for the people who have not been asked to dinner. The ball, which brings us round to breakfast again, is again the ball of our Anglo-Saxon kin beyond the seas. In short, from the society point of view we are in everything their mere rinsings."

"Nothing of the kind!" cried Mrs. Makely. "I won't let you say such a thing! On Thanksgiving-day, too! Why, there is the Thanksgiving dinner itself! If that isn't purely American, I should like to know what is."

"It is purely American, but it is strictly domestic; it is not society. Nobody but some great soul like you, Mrs. Makely, would have the courage to ask anybody to a Thanksgiving dinner, and even you ask only such easy-going house-friends as we are proud to be. You wouldn't think of giving a dinner-party on Thanksgiving?"

"No, I certainly shouldn't. I should think it was very presuming; and you are all as nice as you can be to have come to-day; I am not the only great soul at the table. But that is neither here nor there. Thanksgiving is a purely American thing, and it's more popular than ever. A few years ago you never heard of it outside of New England."

The gentleman laughed. "You are perfectly right, Mrs. Makely, as you always are. Thanksgiving is purely American. So is the corn-husking, so is the apple-bee, so is the sugar-party, so is the spelling-match, so is the church-sociable; but none of these have had their evolution in our society entertainments. The New Year's call was also purely American, but that is now as extinct as the dodo, though I believe the other American festivities are still known in the rural districts."

"Yes," said Mrs. Makely, "and I think it's a great shame that we can't have some of them in a refined form in society. I once went to a sugar-party up in New Hampshire when I was a girl, and I never enjoyed myself so much in my life. I should like to make up a party to go to one somewhere in the Catskills in March. Will you all go? It would be something to show Mr. Homos. I should like to show him something really American before he goes home. There's nothing American left in society!"

"You forget the American woman," suggested the gentleman. "She is always American, and she is always in society."

"Yes," returned our hostess, with a thoughtful air, "you're quite right in that. One always meets more women than men in society. But it's because the men are so lazy, and so comfortable at their clubs, they won't go. They enjoy themselves well enough in society after they get there, as I tell my husband when he grumbles over having to dress."

"Well," said the gentleman, "a great many things, the day-time things, we really can't come to, because we don't belong to the aristocratic class, as you ladies do, and we are busy down - town. But I don't think we are reluctant about dinner; and the young fellows are nearly always willing to go to a ball, if the supper's good and it's a house where they don't feel obliged to dance. But what do *you* think, Mr. Ho-

65

mos?" he asked. "How does your observation coincide with my experience?"

I answered that I hardly felt myself qualified to speak, for though I had assisted at the different kinds of society rites he had mentioned, thanks to the hospitality of my friends in New York, I knew the English functions only from a very brief stay in England on my way here, and from what I had read of them in English fiction and in the relations of our emissaries. He inquired into our emissary system, and the company appeared greatly interested in such account of it as I could briefly give.

"Well," he said, "that would do while you kept it to yourselves; but now that your country is known to the plutocratic world, your public documents will be apt to come back to the countries your emissaries have visited, and make trouble. The first thing you know some of our bright reporters will get on to one of your emissaries, and interview him, and then we shall get what you think of us at first hands. By-the-by, have you seen any of those primitive social delights which Mrs. Makely regrets so much?"

"I!" our hostess protested. But then she perceived that he was joking, and she let me answer.

I said that I had seen them nearly all, during the past year, in New England and in the West, but they appeared to me inalienable of the simpler life of the country, and that I was not surprised they should not have found an evolution in the more artificial society of the cities.

"I see," he returned, "that you reserve your *opinion* of our more artificial society; but you may be sure that our reporters will get it out of you yet before you leave us."

"Those horrid reporters!" one of the ladies irrelevantly sighed.

The gentleman resumed: "In the mean time, I don't mind saying how it strikes me. I think you are quite right about the indigenous American things being adapted only to the simpler life of the country and the smaller towns. It is so everywhere. As soon as people become at all refined they look down upon what is their own as something vulgar. But it is peculiarly so with us. We have nothing national that is not connected with the life of work, and when we begin to live the life of pleasure we must borrow from the people abroad, who have always lived the life of pleasure."

"Mr. Homos, you know," Mrs. Makely explained for me, as if this were the aptest moment, "thinks we all ought to work. He thinks we oughtn't to have any servants."

"Oh no, my dear lady," I put in. "I don't think that of you as you *are*. None of you could see more plainly than I do that in your conditions you *must* have servants, and that you cannot possibly work unless poverty obliges you."

The other ladies had turned upon me with surprise and horror at Mrs. Makely's words, but they now apparently relented, as if I had fully redeemed myself from the charge made against me. Mrs. Strange alone seemed to have found nothing monstrous in my supposed position. "Sometimes," she said, "I wish we had to work, all of us, and that we could be freed from our servile bondage to servants."

Several of the ladies admitted that it was the greatest slavery in the world, and that it would be comparative luxury to do one's own work. But they all asked, in one form or another, what were they to do,

67

and Mrs. Strange owned that she did not know. The facetious gentleman asked me how the ladies did in Altruria, and when I told them, as well as I could, they were, of course, very civil about it, but I could see that they all thought it impossible, or, if not impossible, then ridiculous. I did not feel bound to defend our customs, and I knew very well that each woman there was imagining herself in our conditions with the curse of her plutocratic tradition still upon her. They could not do otherwise, any of them, and they seemed to get tired of such effort as they did make.

Mrs. Makely rose, and the other ladies rose with her, for the Americans follow the English custom in letting the men remain at table after the women have left. But on this occasion I found it varied by a pretty touch from the French custom, and the men, instead of merely standing up while the women filed out, gave each his arm, as far as the drawing-room, to the lady he had brought in to dinner. Then we went back, and what is the pleasantest part of the dinner to most men began for us.

XVI

I MUST say, to the credit of the Americans, that
although the eating and drinking among them appear gross enough to an Altrurian, you are not revolted by the coarse stories which the English sometimes tell as soon as the ladies have left them. If it
is a men's dinner, or more especially a men's supper,
these stories are pretty sure to follow the coffee; but
when there have been women at the board, some sense
of their presence seems to linger in the more delicate
American nerves, and the indulgence is limited to two
or three things off color, as the phrase is here, told
with anxious glances at the drawing-room doors, to see
if they are fast shut.

I do not remember just what brought the talk back
from these primrose paths to that question of American society forms, but presently some one said he
believed the church - sociable was the thing in most
towns beyond the apple-bee and sugar-party stage, and
this opened the inquiry as to how far the church still
formed the social life of the people in cities. Some
one suggested that in Brooklyn it formed it altogether,
and then they laughed, for Brooklyn is always a joke
with the New-Yorkers; I do not know exactly why,
except that this vast city is so largely a suburb, and
that it has a great number of churches and is comparatively cheap. Then another told of a lady who
had come to New York (he admitted, twenty years
ago), and was very lonely, as she had no letters until
she joined a church. This at once brought her a gen-

eral acquaintance, and she began to find herself in society; but as soon as she did so she joined a more exclusive church, where they took no notice of strangers. They all laughed at that bit of human nature, as they called it, and they philosophized the relation of women to society as a purely business relation. The talk ranged to the mutable character of society, and how people got into it, or were of it, and how it was very different from what it once was, except that with women it was always business. They spoke of certain new rich people with affected contempt; but I could see that they were each proud of knowing such millionaires as they could claim for acquaintance, though they pretended to make fun of the number of men - servants you had to run the gantlet of in their houses before you could get to your hostess.

One of my commensals said he had noticed that I took little or no wine, and, when I said that we seldom drank it in Altruria, he answered that he did not think I could make that go in America, if I meant to dine much. "Dining, you know, means overeating," he explained, "and if you wish to overeat you must overdrink. I venture to say that you will pass a worse night than any of us, Mr. Homos, and that you will be sorrier to-morrow than I shall." They were all smoking, and I confess that their tobacco was secretly such an affliction to me that I was at one moment in doubt whether I should take a cigar myself or ask leave to join the ladies.

The gentleman who had talked so much already said: "Well, I don't mind dining, a great deal, especially with Makely, here, but I do object to supping, as I have to do now and then, in the way of pleasure. Last Saturday night I sat down at eleven o'clock to blue-point oysters, consommé, stewed terrapin—yours was very good, Makely; I wish I had taken more of it—lamb chops with pease, redhead duck with celery mayonnaise, Nesselrode pudding, fruit, cheese, and coffee, with sausages, caviare, radishes, celery, and olives interspersed wildly, and drinkables and smokables *ad libitum;* and I can assure you that I felt very devout when I woke up after church-time in the morning. It is this turning night into day that is killing us. We men, who have to go to business the next morning, ought to strike, and say that we won't go to anything later than eight-o'clock dinner."

"Ah, then the women would insist upon our making it four-o'clock tea," said another.

Our host seemed to be reminded of something by the mention of the women, and he said, after a glance at the state of the cigars, "Shall we join the ladies?"

One of the men-servants had evidently been waiting for this question. He held the door open, and we all filed into the drawing-room.

Mrs. Makely hailed me with, "Ah, Mr. Homos, I'm so glad you've come! We poor women have been having a most dismal time!"

"Honestly," asked the funny gentleman, "don't you always, without us?"

"Yes, but this has been worse than usual. Mrs. Strange has been asking us how many people we supposed there were in this city, within five minutes' walk of us, who had no dinner to-day. Do you call that kind?"

"A little more than kin and less than kind, perhaps," the gentleman suggested. "But what does she propose to do about it?"

He turned towards Mrs. Strange, who answered, "Nothing. What does any one propose to do about it?"

71

" Then, why do you think about it ?"

" I don't. It thinks about itself. Do you know that poem of Longfellow's, ' The Challenge ' ?"

" No, I never heard of it."

" Well, it begins in his sweet old way, about some Spanish king who was killed before a city he was besieging, and one of his knights sallies out of the camp and challenges the people of the city, the living and the dead, as traitors. Then the poet breaks off, *apropos de rien:*

> " ' There is a greater army
>   That besets us round with strife,
> A numberless, starving army,
>   At all the gates of life.
> The poverty-stricken millions
>   Who challenge our wine and bread
> And impeach us all for traitors,
>   Both the living and the dead.
> And whenever I sit at the banquet,
>   Where the feast and song are high,
> Amid the mirth and the music
>   I can hear that fearful cry.
>
> " ' And hollow and haggard faces
>   Look into the lighted hall,
> And wasted hands are extended
>   To catch the crumbs that fall.
> For within there is light and plenty,
>   And odors fill the air;
> But without there is cold and darkness,
>   And hunger and despair.
> And there, in the camp of famine,
>   In wind and cold and rain,
> Christ, the great Lord of the Army,
>   Lies dead upon the plain.' "

" Ah," said the facetious gentleman, " that is fine! We really forget how fine Longfellow was. It is so pleasant to hear you quoting poetry, Mrs. Strange! That sort of thing has almost gone out; and it's a pity."

XVII

OUR fashion of offering hospitality on the impulse would be as strange here as offering it without some special inducement for its acceptance. The inducement is, as often as can be, a celebrity or eccentricity of some sort, or some visiting foreigner; and I suppose that I have been a good deal used myself in one quality or the other. But when the thing has been done, fully and guardedly at all points, it does not seem to have been done for pleasure, either by the host or the guest. The dinner is given in payment of another dinner; or out of ambition by people who are striving to get forward in society; or by great social figures who give regularly a certain number of dinners every season. In either case it is eaten from motives at once impersonal and selfish. I do not mean to say that I have not been at many dinners where I felt nothing perfunctory either in host or guest, and where as sweet and gay a spirit ruled as at any of our own simple feasts. Still, I think our main impression of American hospitality would be that it was thoroughly infused with the plutocratic principle, and that it meant business.

I am speaking now of the hospitality of society people, who number, after all, but a few thousands out of the many millions of American people. These millions are so far from being in society, even when they are very comfortable, and on the way to great prosperity, if they are not already greatly prosperous,

73

that if they were suddenly confronted with the best society of the great Eastern cities they would find it almost as strange as so many Altrurians. A great part of them have no conception of entertaining except upon an Altrurian scale of simplicity, and they know nothing and care less for the forms that society people value themselves upon. When they begin, in the ascent of the social scale, to adopt forms, it is still to wear them lightly and with an individual freedom and indifference; it is long before anxiety concerning the social law renders them vulgar.

Yet from highest to lowest, from first to last, one invariable fact characterizes them all, and it may be laid down as an axiom that in a plutocracy the man who needs a dinner is the man who is never asked to dine. I do not say that he is not given a dinner. He is very often given a dinner, and for the most part he is kept from starving to death; but he is not suffered to sit at meat with his host, if the person who gives him a meal can be called his host. His need of the meal stamps him with a hopeless inferiority, and relegates him morally to the company of the swine at their husks, and of Lazarus, whose sores the dogs licked. Usually, of course, he is not physically of such a presence as to fit him for any place in good society short of Abraham's bosom; but even if he were entirely decent, or of an inoffensive shabbiness, it would not be possible for his benefactors, in any grade of society, to ask him to their tables. He is sometimes fed in the kitchen; where the people of the house feed in the kitchen themselves, he is fed at the back door.

We were talking of this the other night at the house of that lady whom Mrs. Makely invited me specially to meet on Thanksgiving-day. It happened then, as it often happens here, that although I was asked to meet her, I saw very little of her. It was not so bad as it sometimes is, for I have been asked to meet people, very informally, and passed the whole evening with them, and yet not exchanged a word with them. Mrs. Makely really gave me a seat next Mrs. Strange at table, and we had some unimportant conversation; but there was a lively little creature vis-à-vis of me, who had a fancy of addressing me so much of her talk that my acquaintance with Mrs. Strange rather languished through the dinner, and she went away so soon after the men rejoined the ladies in the drawing-room that I did not speak to her there. I was rather surprised, then, to receive a note from her a few days later, asking me to dinner; and I finally went, I am ashamed to own, more from curiosity than from any other motive. I had been, in the mean time, thoroughly coached concerning her by Mrs. Makely, whom I told of my invitation, and who said, quite frankly, that she wished Mrs. Strange had asked her, too. "But Eveleth Strange wouldn't do that," she explained, "because it would have the effect of paying me back. I'm so glad, on your account, that you're going, for I do want you to know at least one American woman that you can unreservedly approve of; I know you don't *begin* to approve of *me;* and I was so vexed that you really had no chance to talk with her that night you met her here; it seemed to me as if she ran away early just to provoke me; and, to tell you the truth, I thought she had taken a dislike to you. I wish I could tell you just what sort of a person she is, but it would be perfectly hopeless, for you haven't got the documents, and you never could get them. I used to be at school with her, and even then she wasn't like any of the other girls. She was always so original, and did things from such a high motive, that afterwards, when we were all settled, I was perfectly thunderstruck at her marrying old Bellington Strange, who was twice her age and had nothing but his money; he was not related to the New York Bellingtons at all, and nobody knows how he got the name; nobody ever heard of the Stranges. In fact, people say that he used to be plain Peter B. Strange till he married Eveleth, and she made him drop the Peter and blossom out in the Bellington, so that he could seem to have a social as well as a financial history. People who dislike her insisted that they were not in the least surprised at her marrying him; that the high-motive business was just her pose; and that she had jumped at the chance of getting him. But I always stuck up for her—and I know that she did it for the sake of her family, who were all as poor as poor, and were dependent on her after her father went to smash in his business. She was always as high-strung and romantic as she could be, but I don't believe that even then she would have taken Mr. Strange if there had been anybody else. I don't suppose any one else ever looked at her, for the young men are pretty sharp nowadays, and are not going to marry girls without a cent, when there are so many rich girls, just as charming every way; you can't expect them to. At any rate, whatever her motive was, she had her reward, for Mr. Strange died within a year of their marriage, and she got all his money. There was no attempt to break the will, for Mr. Strange seemed to be literally of no family; and she's lived quietly on in the house he bought her ever since, except when she's in Europe, and that's about two-thirds of the time. She has her mother with her, and I suppose that her sisters and her cousins and her aunts come in for outdoor aid.

She's always helping somebody. They say that's her pose, now; but, if it is, I don't think it's a bad one; and certainly, if she wanted to get married again, there would be no trouble, with her three millions. I advise you to go to her dinner, by all means, Mr. Homos. It will be something worth while, in every way, and perhaps you'll convert her to Altrurianism; she's as hopeful a subject as *I* know."

XVIII

I WAS one of the earliest of the guests, for I cannot yet believe that people do not want me to come exactly when they say they do. I perceived, however, that one other gentleman had come before me, and I was both surprised and delighted to find that this was my acquaintance Mr. Bullion, the Boston banker. He professed as much pleasure at our meeting as I certainly felt; but after a few words he went on talking with Mrs. Strange, while I was left to her mother, an elderly woman of quiet and even timid bearing, who affected me at once as born and bred in a wholly different environment. In fact, every American of the former generation is almost as strange to it in tradition, though not in principle, as I am; and I found myself singularly at home with this sweet lady, who seemed glad of my interest in her. I was taken from her side to be introduced to a lady, on the opposite side of the room, who said she had been promised my acquaintance by a friend of hers, whom I had met in the mountains—Mr. Twelvemough; did I remember him? She gave a little cry while still speaking, and dramatically stretched her hand towards a gentleman who entered at the moment, and whom I saw to be no other than Mr. Twelvemough himself. As soon as he had greeted our hostess he hastened up to us, and, barely giving himself time to press the still outstretched hand of my companion, shook mine warmly, and expressed the greatest joy at seeing me. He said that he had just got back to town, in a manner, and had not known I was here, till Mrs. Strange had asked him to meet me. There were not a great many other guests, when they all arrived, and we sat down, a party not much larger than at Mrs. Makely's.

I found that I was again to take out my hostess, but I was put next the lady with whom I had been talking; she had come without her husband, who was, apparently, of a different social taste from herself, and had an engagement of his own; there was an artist and his wife, whose looks I liked; some others whom I need not specify were there, I fancied, because they had heard of Altruria and were curious to see me. As Mr. Twelvemough sat quite at the other end of the table, the lady on my right could easily ask me whether I liked his books. She said, tentatively, people liked them because they felt sure when they took up one of his novels they had not got hold of a tract on political economy in disguise.

It was this complimentary close of a remark, which scarcely began with praise, that made itself heard across the table, and was echoed with a heartfelt sigh from the lips of another lady.

"Yes," she said, "that is what I find such a comfort in Mr. Twelvemough's books."

"We were *speaking* of Mr. Twelvemough's books," the first lady triumphed, and several began to extol them for being fiction pure and simple, and not dealing with anything but loves of young people.

Mr. Twelvemough sat looking as modest as he could under the praise, and one of the ladies said that in a novel she had lately read there was a description of a surgical operation that made her feel as if she had been present at a clinic. Then the author said that he had read that passage, too, and found it extreme-

6   79

ly well done. It was fascinating, but it was not art.

The painter asked, Why was it not art?

The author answered, Well, if such a thing as that was art, then anything that a man chose to do in a work of imagination was art.

" Precisely," said the painter—" art *is* choice."

" On that ground," the banker interposed, " you could say that political economy was a fit subject for art, if an artist chose to treat it."

" It would have its difficulties," the painter admitted, " but there are certain phases of political economy, dramatic moments, human moments, which might be very fitly treated in art. For instance, who would object to Mr. Twelvemough's describing an eviction from an East Side tenement-house on a cold winter night, with the mother and her children huddled about the fire the father had kindled with pieces of the household furniture?"

" *I* should object very much, for one," said the lady who had objected to the account of the surgical operation. " It would be too creepy. Art should give pleasure."

" Then you think a tragedy is not art?" asked the painter.

" I think that these harrowing subjects are brought in altogether too much," said the lady. " There are enough of them in real life, without filling all the novels with them. It's terrible the number of beggars you meet on the street, this winter. Do you want to meet them in Mr. Twelvemough's novels, too?"

" Well, it wouldn't cost me any money there. I shouldn't have to give."

" You oughtn't to give money in real life," said the lady. " You ought to give charity tickets. If the beggars refuse them, it shows they are impostors."

"It's some comfort to know that the charities are so active," said the elderly young lady, "even if half the letters one gets *do* turn out to be appeals from them."

"It's very disappointing to have them do it, though," said the artist, lightly. "I thought there was a society to abolish poverty. That doesn't seem to be so active as the charities this winter. Is it possible they've found it a failure?"

"Well," said Mr. Bullion, "perhaps they have suspended during the hard times."

They tossed the ball back and forth with a lightness the Americans have, and I could not have believed, if I had not known how hardened people become to such things here, that they were almost in the actual presence of hunger and cold. It was within five minutes' walk of their warmth and surfeit; and if they had lifted the window and called, "Who goes there?" the houselessness that prowls the night could have answered them from the street below, "Despair!"

"I had an amusing experience," Mr. Twelvemough began, "when I was doing a little visiting for the charities in our ward, the other winter."

"For the sake of the literary material?" the artist suggested.

"Partly for the sake of the literary material; you know we have to look for our own everywhere. But we had a case of an old actor's son, who had got out of all the places he had filled, on account of rheumatism, and could not go to sea, or drive a truck, or even wrap gas-fixtures in paper any more."

"A checkered employ," the banker mused aloud.

"It was not of a simultaneous nature," the novelist

explained. "So he came on the charities, and, as I knew the theatrical profession a little, and how generous it was with all related to it, I said that I would undertake to look after his case. You know the theory is that we get work for our patients, or clients, or whatever they are, and I went to a manager whom I knew to be a good fellow, and I asked him for some sort of work. He said, Yes, send the man round, and he would give him a job copying parts for a new play he had written."

The novelist paused, and nobody laughed.

"It seems to me that your experience is instructive, rather than amusing," said the banker. "It shows that something can be done, if you try."

"Well," said Mr. Twelvemongh, "I thought that was the moral, myself, till the fellow came afterwards to thank me. He said that he considered himself very lucky, for the manager had told him that there were six other men had wanted that job."

Everybody laughed now, and I looked at my hostess in a little bewilderment. She murmured, "I suppose the joke is that he had befriended one man at the expense of six others."

"Oh," I returned, "is that a joke?"

No one answered, but the lady at my right asked, "How do you manage with poverty in Altruria?"

I saw the banker fix a laughing eye on me, but I answered, "In Altruria we have no poverty."

"Ah, I knew you would say that!" he cried out. "That's what he always does," he explained to the lady. "Bring up any one of our little difficulties, and ask how they get over it in Altruria, and he says they have nothing like it. It's very simple."

They all began to ask me questions, but with a courteous incredulity which I could feel well enough,

82

and some of my answers made them laugh, all but my hostess, who received them with a gravity that finally prevailed. But I was not disposed to go on talking of Altruria then, though they all protested a real interest, and murmured against the hardship of being cut off with so brief an account of our country as I had given them.

"Well," said the banker at last, "if there is no cure for our poverty, we might as well go on and enjoy ourselves."

"Yes," said our hostess, with a sad little smile, "we might as well enjoy ourselves."

XIX

THE talk at Mrs. Strange's table took a far wider range than my meagre notes would intimate, and we sat so long that it was almost eleven before the men joined the ladies in the drawing-room. You will hardly conceive of remaining two, three, or four hours at dinner, as one often does here, in society; out of society the meals are despatched with a rapidity unknown to the Altrurians. Our habit of listening to lectors, especially at the evening repast, and then of reasoning upon what we have heard, prolongs our stay at the board; but the fondest listener, the greatest talker among us, would be impatient of the delay eked out here by the great number and the slow procession of the courses served. Yet the poorest American would find his ideal realized rather in the long-drawn-out gluttony of the society dinner here than in our temperate simplicity.

At such a dinner it is very hard to avoid a surfeit, and I have to guard myself very carefully, lest, in the excitement of the talk, I gorge myself with everything, in its turn. Even at the best, my overloaded stomach often joins with my conscience in reproaching me for what you would think a shameful excess at table. Yet, wicked as my riot is, my waste is worse, and I have to think, with contrition, not only of what I have eaten, but of what I have left uneaten, in a city where so many wake and sleep in hunger.

The ladies made a show of lingering after we joined

them in the drawing-room; but there were furtive glances at the clock, and presently her guests began to bid Mrs. Strange good-night. When I came up and offered her my hand, she would not take it, but murmured, with a kind of passion: "Don't go! I mean it! Stay, and tell us about Altruria—my mother and me!"

I was by no means loath, for I must confess that all I had seen and heard of this lady interested me in her more and more. I felt at home with her, too, as with no other society woman I have met; she seemed to me not only good, but very sincere, and very good-hearted, in spite of the world she lived in. Yet I have met so many disappointments here, of the kind that our civilization wholly fails to prepare us for, that I should not have been surprised to find that Mrs. Strange had wished me to stay, not that she might hear me talk about Altruria, but that I might hear her talk about herself. You must understand that the essential vice of a system which concentres a human being's thoughts upon his own interests, from the first moment of responsibility, colors and qualifies every motive with egotism. All egotists are unconscious, for otherwise they would be intolerable to themselves; but some are subtler than others; and as most women have finer natures than most men everywhere, and in America most women have finer minds than most men, their egotism usually takes the form of pose. This is usually obvious, but in some cases it is so delicately managed that you do not suspect it, unless some other woman gives you a hint of it, and even then you cannot be sure of it, seeing the self-sacrifice, almost to martyrdom, which the *poseuse* makes for it. If Mrs. Makely had not suggested that some people attributed a pose to Mrs. Strange, I should certainly never have

85

dreamed of looking for it, and I should have been only intensely interested, when she began, as soon as I was left alone with her and her mother:

"You may not know how unusual I am in asking this favor of you, Mr. Homos; but you might as well learn from me as from others that I am rather unusual in everything. In fact, you can report in Altruria, when you get home, that you found at least one woman in America whom fortune had smiled upon in every way, and who hated her smiling fortune almost as much as she hated herself. I'm quite satisfied," she went on, with a sad mockery, "that fortune is a man, and an American; when he has given you all the materials for having a good time, he believes that you must be happy, because there is nothing to hinder. It isn't that I want to be happy in the greedy way that men think we do, for then I could easily be happy. If you have a soul which is not above buttons, buttons are enough. But if you expect to be of real use, to help on, and to help out, you will be disappointed. I have not the faith that they say upholds you Altrurians in trying to help out, if I don't see my way out. It seems to me that my reason has some right to satisfaction, and that, if I am a woman grown, I can't be satisfied with the assurances they would give to little girls—that everything is going on well. Any one can see that things are not going on well. There is more and more wretchedness of every kind, not hunger of body alone, but hunger of soul. If you escape one, you suffer the other, because, if you *have* a soul, you must long to help, not for a time, but for all time. I suppose," she asked, abruptly, "that Mrs. Makely has told you something about me?"

"Something," I admitted.

"I ask," she went on, "because I don't want to

bore you with a statement of my case, if you know
it already. Ever since I heard you were in New York
I have wished to see you, and to talk with you about
Altruria; I did not suppose that there would be any
chance at Mrs. Makely's, and there wasn't; and I did
not suppose there would be any chance here, unless I
could take courage to do what I have done now. You
must excuse it, if it seems as extraordinary a proceed-
ing to you as it really is; I wouldn't at all have you
think it is usual for a lady to ask one of her guests to
stay after the rest, in order, if you please, to confess
herself to him. It's a crime without a name."

She laughed, not gayly, but humorously, and then
went on, speaking always with a feverish eagerness
which I find it hard to give you a sense of, for the
women here have an intensity quite beyond our experience of the sex at home.

"But you are a foreigner, and you come from an
order of things so utterly unlike ours that perhaps
you will be able to condone my offence. At any rate,
I have risked it." She laughed again, more gayly,
and recovered herself in a cheerfuller and easier mood.
"Well, the long and the short of it is that I have
come to the end of my tether. I have tried, as truly
as I believe any woman ever did, to do my share, with
money and with work, to help make life better for
those whose life is bad; and though one mustn't boast
of good works, I may say that I have been pretty
thorough, and, if I've given up, it's because I see, in
our state of things, *no* hope of curing the evil. It's
like trying to soak up the drops of a rainstorm. You
do dry up a drop here and there; but the clouds are
full of them, and, the first thing you know, you stand,
with your blotting-paper in your hand, in a puddle
over your shoe-tops. There is nothing but charity, and

charity is a failure, except for the moment. If you think of the misery around you, that must remain around you for ever and ever, as long as you live, you have your choice—to go mad and be put into an asylum, or go mad and devote yourself to society."

XX

WHILE Mrs. Strange talked on, her mother listened quietly, with a dim, submissive smile and her hands placidly crossed in her lap. She now said:

"It seems to be very different now from what it was in my time. There are certainly a great many beggars, and we used never to have one. Children grew up, and people lived and died, in large towns, without ever seeing one. I remember, when my husband first took me abroad, how astonished we were at the beggars. Now I meet as many in New York as I met in London or in Rome. But if you don't do charity, what can you do? Christ enjoined it, and Paul says—"

"Oh, people *never* do the charity that Christ meant," said Mrs. Strange; "and, as things are now, how *could* they? Who would dream of dividing half her frocks and wraps with poor women, or selling *all* and giving to the poor? That is what makes it so hopeless. We *know* that Christ was perfectly right, and that He was perfectly sincere in what He said to the good young millionaire; but we all go away exceeding sorrowful, just as the good young millionaire did. We have to, if we don't want to come on charity ourselves. How do *you* manage about that?" she asked me; and then she added, "But, of course, I forgot that you have no need of charity."

"Oh yes, we have," I returned; and I tried, once more, as I have tried so often with Americans, to explain how the heavenly need of giving the self continues with us, but on terms that do not harrow the conscience of the giver, as self-sacrifice always must here, at its purest and noblest. I sought to make her conceive of our nation as a family, where every one was secured against want by the common provision, and against the degrading and depraving inequality which comes from want. The " dead-level of equality " is what the Americans call the condition in which all would be as the angels of God, and they blasphemously deny that He ever meant His creatures to be alike happy, because some, through a long succession of unfair advantages, have inherited more brain or brawn or beauty than others. I found that this gross and impious notion of God darkened even the clear intelligence of a woman like Mrs. Strange; and, indeed, it prevails here so commonly that it is one of the first things advanced as an argument against the Altrurianization of America.

I believe I did, at last, succeed in showing her how charity still continues among us, but in forms that bring neither a sense of inferiority to him who takes nor anxiety to him who gives. I said that benevolence here often seemed to involve, essentially, some such risk as a man should run if he parted with a portion of the vital air which belonged to himself and his family, in succoring a fellow-being from suffocation; but that with us, where it was no more possible for one to deprive himself of his share of the common food, shelter, and clothing, than of the air he breathed, one could devote one's self utterly to others without that foul alloy of fear which I thought must basely qualify every good deed in plutocratic conditions.

She said that she knew what I meant, and that I was quite right in my conjecture, as regarded men, at least; a man who did not stop to think what the effect, upon himself and his own, his giving must have, would be a fool or a madman; but women could often give as recklessly as they spent, without any thought of consequences, for they did not know how money came.

"Women," I said, "are exterior to your conditions, and they can sacrifice themselves without wronging any one."

"Or, rather," she continued, "without the sense of wronging any one. Our men like to keep us in that innocence or ignorance; they think it is pretty, or they think it is funny; and as long as a girl is in her father's house, or a wife is in her husband's, she knows no more of money-earning or money-making than a child. Most grown women among us, if they had a sum of money in the bank, would not know how to get it out. They would not know how to indorse a check, much less draw one. But there are plenty of women who are inside the conditions, as much as men are— poor women who have to earn their bread, and rich women who have to manage their property. I can't speak for the poor women; but I can speak for the rich, and I can confess for them that what you imagine is true. The taint of unfaith and distrust is on every dollar that you dole out, so that, as far as the charity of the rich is concerned, I would read Shakespeare:

"It curseth him that gives, and him that takes."

"Perhaps that is why the rich give comparatively so little. The poor can never understand how much the rich value their money, how much the owner of a great fortune dreads to see it less. If it were not so, they would surely give more than they do; for a man

91

who has ten millions could give eight of them without feeling the loss; the man with a hundred could give ninety and be no nearer want. Ah, it's a strange mystery! My poor husband and I used to talk of it a great deal, in the long year that he lay dying; and I think I hate my superfluity the more because I know he hated it so much."

A little trouble had stolen into her impassioned tones, and there was a gleam, as of tears, in the eyes she dropped for a moment. They were shining still when she lifted them again to mine.

" I suppose," she said, " that Mrs. Makely told you something of my marriage ?"

" Eveleth !" her mother protested, with a gentle murmur.

" Oh, I think I can be frank with Mr. Homos. He is not an American, and he will understand, or, at least, he will not misunderstand. Besides, I dare say I shall not say anything worse than Mrs. Makely has said already. My husband was much older than I, and I ought not to have married him; a young girl ought never to marry an old man, or even a man who is only a good many years her senior. But we both faithfully tried to make the best of our mistake, not the worst, and I think this effort helped us to respect each other, when there couldn't be any question of more. He was a rich man, and he had made his money out of nothing, or, at least, from a beginning of utter poverty. But in his last years he came to a sense of its worthlessness, such as few men who have made their money ever have. He was a common man, in a great many ways; he was imperfectly educated, and he was ungrammatical, and he never was at home in society; but he had a tender heart and an honest nature, and I revere his memory, as no one would believe I could

92

without knowing him as I did. His money became a burden and a terror to him; he did not know what to do with it, and he was always morbidly afraid of doing harm with it; he got to thinking that money was an evil in itself."

"That is what we think," I ventured.

"Yes, I know. But he had thought this out for himself, and yet he had times when his thinking about it seemed to him a kind of craze, and, at any rate, he distrusted himself so much that he died leaving it all to me. I suppose he thought that perhaps I could learn how to give it without hurting; and then he knew that, in our state of things, I must have some money to keep the wolf from the door. And I am afraid to part with it, too. I have given and given; but there seems some evil spell on the principal that guards it from encroachment, so that it remains the same, and, if I do not watch, the interest grows in the bank, with that frightful life dead money seems endowed with, as the hair of dead people grows in the grave."

"Eveleth!" her mother murmured again.

"Oh yes," she answered, "I dare say my words are wild. I dare say they only mean that I loathe my luxury from the bottom of my soul, and long to be rid of it, if I only could, without harm to others and with safety to myself."

XXI

It seemed to me that I became suddenly sensible of this luxury for the first time. I had certainly been aware that I was in a large and stately house, and that I had been served and banqueted with a princely pride and profusion. But there had, somehow, been through all a sort of simplicity, a sort of quiet, so that I had not thought of the establishment and its operation, even so much as I had thought of Mrs. Makely's far inferior scale of living; or else, what with my going about so much in society, I was ceasing to be so keenly observant of the material facts as I had been at first. But I was better qualified to judge of what I saw, and I had now a vivid sense of the costliness of Mrs. Strange's environment. There were thousands of dollars in the carpets underfoot; there were tens of thousands in the pictures on the walls. In a bronze group that withdrew itself into a certain niche, with a faint relucence, there was the value of a skilled artisan's wage for five years of hard work; in the bindings of the books that showed from the library shelves there was almost as much money as most of the authors had got for writing them. Every fixture, every movable, was an artistic masterpiece; a fortune, as fortunes used to be counted even in this land of affluence, had been lavished in the mere furnishing of a house which the palaces of nobles and princes of other times had contributed to embellish.

"My husband," Mrs. Strange went on, "bought this

94

house for me, and let me furnish it after my own fancy. After it was all done we neither of us liked it, and when he died I felt as if he had left me in a tomb here."

"Eveleth," said her mother, "you ought not to speak so before Mr. Homos. He will not know what to think of you, and he will go back to Altruria with a very wrong idea of American women."

At this protest, Mrs. Strange seemed to recover herself a little. "Yes," she said, "you must excuse me. I have no right to speak so. But one is often much franker with foreigners than with one's own kind, and, besides, there is something—I don't know what—that will not let me keep the truth from you."

She gazed at me entreatingly, and then, as if some strong emotion swept her from her own hold, she broke out:

"He thought he would make some sort of atonement to me, as if I owed none to him! His money was all he had to do it with, and he spent that upon me in every way he could think of, though he knew that money could not buy anything that was really good, and that, if it bought anything beautiful, it uglified it with the sense of cost to every one who could value it in dollars and cents. He was a good man, far better than people ever imagined, and very simple-hearted and honest, like a child, in his contrition for his wealth, which he did not dare to get rid of; and though I know that, if he were to come back, it would be just as it was, his memory is as dear to me as if—"

She stopped, and pressed in her lip with her teeth, to stay its tremor. I was painfully affected. I knew that she had never meant to be so open with me, and was shocked and frightened at herself. I was sorry for her, and yet I was glad, for it seemed to me that she had given me a glimpse, not only of the truth in her own heart, but of the truth in the hearts of a whole order of prosperous people in these lamentable conditions, whom I shall hereafter be able to judge more leniently, more justly.

I began to speak of Altruria, as if that were what our talk had been leading up to, and she showed herself more intelligently interested concerning us than any one I have yet seen in this country. We appeared, I found, neither incredible nor preposterous to her; our life, in her eyes, had that beauty of right living which the Americans so feebly imagine or imagine not at all. She asked what route I had come by to America, and she seemed disappointed and aggrieved that we placed the restrictions we have felt necessary upon visitors from the plutocratic world. Were we afraid, she asked, that they would corrupt our citizens or mar our content with our institutions? She seemed scarcely satisfied when I explained, as I have explained so often here, that the measures we had taken were rather in the interest of the plutocratic world than of the Altrurians; and alleged the fact that no visitor from the outside had ever been willing to go home again, as sufficient proof that we had nothing to fear from the spread of plutocratic ideals among us. I assured her, and this she easily imagined, that, the better known these became, the worse they appeared to us; and that the only concern our priors felt, in regard to them, was that our youth could not conceive of them in their enormity, but, in seeing how estimable plutocratic people often were, they would attribute to their conditions the inherent good of human nature. I said our own life was so directly reasoned from its economic premises that they could hardly believe the plutocratic life was often an absolute *non sequitur* of the plutocratic premises. I confessed that this error was at the bottom of my own wish to visit America and study those premises.

"And what has your conclusion been?" she said, leaning eagerly towards me, across the table between us, laden with the maps and charts we had been examining for the verification of the position of Altruria, and my own course here, by way of England.

A slight sigh escaped Mrs. Gray, which I interpreted as an expression of fatigue; it was already past twelve o'clock, and I made it the pretext for escape.

"You have seen the meaning and purport of Altruria so clearly," I said, "that I think I can safely leave you to guess the answer to that question."

She laughed, and did not try to detain me now when I offered my hand for good-night. I fancied her mother took leave of me coldly, and with a certain effect of inculpation.

XXII

It is long since I wrote you, and you have had reason enough to be impatient of my silence. I submit to the reproaches of your letter, with a due sense of my blame; whether I am altogether to blame, you shall say after you have read this.

I cannot yet decide whether I have lost a great happiness, the greatest that could come to any man, or escaped the worst misfortune that could befall me. But, such as it is, I will try to set the fact honestly down.

I do not know whether you had any conjecture, from my repeated mention of a lady whose character greatly interested me, that I was in the way of feeling any other interest in her than my letters expressed. I am no longer young, though at thirty-five an Altrurian is by no means so old as an American at the same age. The romantic ideals of the American women which I had formed from the American novels had been dissipated; if I had any sentiment towards them, as a type, it was one of distrust, which my very sense of the charm in their inconsequence, their beauty, their brilliancy, served rather to intensify. I thought myself doubly defended by that difference between their civilization and ours which forbade reasonable hope of happiness in any sentiment for them tenderer than that of the student of strange effects in human nature. But we have not yet, my dear Cyril, reasoned the passions, even in Altruria.

After I last wrote you, a series of accidents, or what appeared so, threw me more and more constantly into the society of Mrs. Strange. We began to laugh at the fatality with which we met everywhere — at teas, at lunches, at dinners, at evening receptions, and even at balls, where I have been a great deal, because, with all my thirty-five years, I have not yet outlived that fondness for dancing which has so often amused you in me. Wherever my acquaintance widened among cultivated people, they had no inspiration but to ask us to meet each other, as if there were really no other woman in New York who could be expected to understand me. "You must come to lunch (or tea, or dinner, whichever it might be), and we will have her. She will be so much interested to meet you."

But perhaps we should have needed none of these accidents to bring us together. I, at least, can look back and see that, when none of them happened, I sought occasions for seeing her, and made excuses of our common interest in this matter and in that to go to her. As for her, I can only say that I seldom failed to find her at home, whether I called upon her nominal day or not, and more than once the man who let me in said he had been charged by Mrs. Strange to say that, if I called, she was to be back very soon; or else he made free to suggest that, though Mrs. Strange was not at home, Mrs. Gray was; and then I found it easy to stay until Mrs. Strange returned. The good old lady had an insatiable curiosity about Altruria, and, though I do not think she ever quite believed in our reality, she at least always treated me kindly, as if I were the victim of an illusion that was thoroughly benign.

I think she had some notion that your letters, which I used often to take with me and read to Mrs. Strange and herself, were inventions of mine; and the fact that they bore only an English postmark confirmed her in this notion, though I explained that in our present passive attitude towards the world outside we had as yet no postal relations with other countries, and, as all our communication at home was by electricity, that we had no letter-post of our own. The very fact that she belonged to a purer and better age in America disqualified her to conceive of Altruria; her daughter, who had lived into a full recognition of the terrible anarchy in which the conditions have ultimated here, could far more vitally imagine us, and to her, I believe, we were at once a living reality. Her perception, her sympathy, her intelligence, became more and more to me, and I escaped to them oftener and oftener, from a world where an Altrurian must be so painfully at odds. In all companies here I am aware that I have been regarded either as a good joke or a bad joke, according to the humor of the listener, and it was grateful to be taken seriously.

From the first I was sensible of a charm in her, different from that I felt in other American women, and impossible in our Altrurian women. She had a deep and almost tragical seriousness, masked with a most winning gayety, a light irony, a fine scorn that was rather for herself than for others. She had thought herself out of all sympathy with her environment; she knew its falsehood, its vacuity, its hopelessness; but she necessarily remained in it and of it. She was as much at odds in it as I was, without my poor privilege of criticism and protest, for, as she said, she could not set herself up as a censor of things that she must keep on doing as other people did. She could have renounced the world, as there are ways and means of doing here; but she had no vocation to the

100

religious life, and she could not feign it without a sense of sacrilege. In fact, this generous and magnanimous and gifted woman was without that faith, that trust in God which comes to us from living His law, and which I wonder any American can keep. She denied nothing; but she had lost the strength to affirm anything. She no longer tried to do good from her heart, though she kept on doing charity in what she said was a mere mechanical impulse from the belief of other days, but always with the ironical doubt that she was doing harm. Women are nothing by halves, as men can be, and she was in a despair which no man can realize, for we have always some if or and which a woman of the like mood casts from her in wild rejection. Where she could not clearly see her way to a true life, it was the same to her as an impenetrable darkness.

You will have inferred something of all this from what I have written of her before, and from words of hers that I have reported to you. Do you think it so wonderful, then, that in the joy I felt at the hope, the solace, which my story of our life seemed to give her, she should become more and more precious to me? It was not wonderful, either, I think, that she should identify me with that hope, that solace, and should suffer herself to lean upon me, in a reliance infinitely sweet and endearing. But what a fantastic dream it now appears!

XXIII

I CAN hardly tell you just how we came to own our love to each other; but one day I found myself alone with her mother, with the sense that Eveleth had suddenly withdrawn from the room at the knowledge of my approach. Mrs. Gray was strongly moved by something; but she governed herself, and, after giving me a tremulous hand, bade me sit.

"Will you excuse me, Mr. Homos," she began, "if I ask you whether you intend to make America your home after this?"

"Oh no!" I answered, and I tried to keep out of my voice the despair with which the notion filled me. I have sometimes had nightmares here, in which I thought that I was an American by choice, and I can give you no conception of the rapture of awakening to the fact that I could still go back to Altruria, that I had not cast my lot with this wretched people. "How could I do that?" I faltered; and I was glad to perceive that I had imparted to her no hint of the misery which I had felt at such a notion.

"I mean, by getting naturalized, and becoming a citizen, and taking up your residence among us."

"No," I answered, as quietly as I could, "I had not thought of that."

"And you still intend to go back to Altruria?"

"I hope so; I ought to have gone back long ago, and if I had not met the friends I have in this house—"

I stopped, for I did not know how I should end what I had begun to say.

" I am glad you think we are your friends," said the lady, " for we have tried to show ourselves your friends. I feel as if this had given me the right to say something to you that you may think very odd."

" Say anything to me, my dear lady," I returned. " I shall not think it unkind, no matter how odd it is."

" Oh, it's nothing. It's merely that—that when you are not here with us I lose my grasp on Altruria, and —and I begin to doubt—"

I smiled. " I know! People here have often hinted something of that kind to me. Tell me, Mrs. Gray, do Americans generally take me for an impostor ?"

" Oh no!" she answered, fervently. " Everybody that I have heard speak of you has the highest regard for you, and believes you perfectly sincere. But—"

" But what ?" I entreated.

" They think you may be mistaken."

" Then they think I am out of my wits—that I am in an hallucination !"

" No, not that," she returned. " But it is so very difficult for us to conceive of a whole nation living, as you say you do, on the same terms as one family, and no one trying to get ahead of another, or richer, and having neither inferiors nor superiors, but just one dead level of equality, where there is no distinction except by natural gifts and good deeds or beautiful works. It seems impossible—it seems ridiculous."

" Yes," I confessed, " I know that it seems so to the Americans."

" And I must tell you something else, Mr. Homos, and I hope you won't take it amiss. The first night when you talked about Altruria here, and showed us how you had come, by way of England, and the place where Altruria ought to be on our maps, I looked them over, after you were gone, and I could make nothing of it. I have often looked at the map since, but I could never find Altruria; it was no use."

"Why," I said, " if you will let me have your atlas—"

She shook her head. "It would be the same again as soon as you went away." I could not conceal my distress, and she went on: " Now, you mustn't mind what I say. I'm nothing but a silly old woman, and Eveleth would never forgive me if she could know what I've been saying."

" Then Mrs. Strange isn't troubled, as you are, concerning me ?" I asked, and I confess my anxiety attenuated my voice almost to a whisper.

" She won't admit that she is. It might be better for her if she would. But Eveleth is very true to her friends, and that—that makes me all the more anxious that she should not deceive herself."

" Oh, Mrs. Gray !" I could not keep a certain tone of reproach out of my words.

She began to weep. " There ! I knew I should hurt your feelings. But you mustn't mind what I say. I beg your pardon ! I take it all back—"

" Ah, I don't want you to take it back ! But what proof shall I give you that there is such a land as Altruria ? If the darkness implies the day, America must imply Altruria. In what way do I seem false, or mad, except that I claim to be the citizen of a country where people love one another as the first Christians did ?"

" That is just it," she returned. " Nobody can imagine the first Christians, and do you think we can imagine anything like them in our own day ?"

" But Mrs. Strange—she imagines us, you say ?"

104

" She thinks she does; but I am afraid she only thinks so, and I know her better than you do, Mr. Homos. I know how enthusiastic she always was, and how unhappy she has been since she has lost her hold on faith, and how eagerly she has caught at the hope you have given her of a higher life on earth than we live here. If she should ever find out that she was wrong, I don't know what would become of her. You mustn't mind me; you mustn't let me wound you by what I say."

" You don't wound me, and I only thank you for what you say; but I entreat you to believe in me. Mrs. Strange has not deceived herself, and I have not deceived her. Shall I protest to you, by all I hold sacred, that I am really what I told you I was; that I am not less, and that Altruria is infinitely more, happier, better, gladder, than any words of mine can say? Shall I not have the happiness to see your daughter to-day? I had something to say to her—and now I have so much more! If she is in the house, won't you send to her? I can make her understand—"

I stopped at a certain expression which I fancied I saw in Mrs. Gray's face.

" Mr. Homos," she began, so very seriously that my heart trembled with a vague misgiving, " sometimes I think you had better not see my daughter any more."

" Not see her any more?" I gasped.

" Yes; I don't see what good can come of it, and it's all very strange and uncanny. I don't know how to explain it; but, indeed, it isn't anything personal. It's because you are of a state of things so utterly opposed to human nature that I don't see how—I am afraid that—"

" But I am not uncanny to *her!*" I entreated. " I am not unnatural, not incredible—"

105

"Oh no; that is the worst of it. But I have said too much; I have said a great deal more than I ought. But you must excuse it: I am an old woman. I am not very well, and I suppose it's that that makes me talk so much."

She rose from her chair, and I, perforce, rose from mine and made a movement towards her.

"No, no," she said, "I don't need any help. You must come again soon and see us, and show that you've forgotten what I've said." She gave me her hand, and I could not help bending over it and kissing it. She gave a little, pathetic whimper. "Oh, I *know* I've said the most dreadful things to you."

"You haven't said anything that takes your friendship from me, Mrs. Gray, and that is what I care for." My own eyes filled with tears—I do not know why—and I groped my way from the room. Without seeing any one in the obscurity of the hallway, where I found myself, I was aware of some one there, by that sort of fine perception which makes us know the presence of a spirit.

"You are going?" a whisper said. "Why are you going?" And Eveleth had me by the hand and was drawing me gently into the dim drawing-room that opened from the place. "I don't know all my mother has been saying to you. I had to let her say something; she thought she ought. I knew you would know how to excuse it."

"Oh, my dearest!" I said, and why I said this I do not know, or how we found ourselves in each other's arms.

"What are we doing?" she murmured.

"You don't believe I am an impostor, an illusion, a visionary?" I besought her, straining her closer to my heart.

106

" I believe in you, with all my soul!" she answered.

We sat down, side by side, and talked long. I did not go away the whole day. With a high disdain of convention, she made me stay. Her mother sent word that she would not be able to come to dinner, and we were alone together at table, in an image of what our united lives might be. We spent the evening in that happy interchange of trivial confidences that lovers use in symbol of the unutterable raptures that fill them. We were there in what seemed an infinite present, without a past, without a future.

XXIV

SOCIETY had to be taken into our confidence, and Mrs. Makely saw to it that there were no reserves with society. Our engagement was not quite like that of two young persons, but people found in our character and circumstance an interest far transcending that felt in the engagement of the most romantic lovers. Some note of the fact came to us by accident, as one evening when we stood near a couple and heard them talking. " It must be very weird," the man said; " something like being engaged to a materialization." " Yes," said the girl, " quite the Demon Lover business, I should think." She glanced round, as people do, in talking, and, at sight of us, she involuntarily put her hand over her mouth. I looked at Eveleth; there was nothing expressed in her face but a generous anxiety for me. But so far as the open attitude of society towards us was concerned, nothing could have been more flattering. We could hardly have been more asked to meet each other than before; but now there were entertainments in special recognition of our betrothal, which Eveleth said could not be altogether refused, though she found the ordeal as irksome as I did. In America, however, you get used to many things. I do not know why it should have been done, but in the society columns of several of the great newspapers our likenesses were printed, from photographs procured I cannot guess how, with descriptions of our persons as to those points of coloring and carriage and stature which the pictures could not give, and with biographies such as could be ascertained in her case and imagined in mine. In some of the society papers, paragraphs of a surprising scurrility appeared, attacking me as an impostor, and aspersing the motives of Eveleth in her former marriage, and treating her as a foolish crank or an audacious flirt. The goodness of her life, her self-sacrifice and works of benevolence, counted for no more against these wanton attacks than the absolute inoffensiveness of my own; the writers knew no harm of her, and they knew nothing at all of me; but they devoted us to the execration of their readers simply because we formed apt and ready themes for paragraphs. You may judge of how wild they were in their aim when some of them denounced me as an Altrurian plutocrat!

We could not escape this storm of notoriety; we had simply to let it spend its fury. When it began, several reporters of both sexes came to interview me, and questioned me, not only as to all the facts of my past life, and all my purposes in the future, but as to my opinion of hypnotism, eternal punishment, the Ibsen drama, and the tariff reform. I did my best to answer them seriously, and certainly I answered them civilly; but it seemed from what they printed that the answers I gave did not concern them, for they gave others for me. They appeared to me for the most part kindly and well-meaning young people, though vastly ignorant of vital things. They had apparently visited me with minds made up, or else their reports were revised by some controlling hand, and a quality injected more in the taste of the special journals they represented than in keeping with the facts. When I realized this, I refused to see any more reporters, or to answer them, and then they printed the questions they had prepared to ask me, in such form that my silence was made of the same damaging effect as a full confession of guilt upon the charges.

The experience was so strange and new to me that it affected me in a degree I was unwilling to let Eveleth imagine. But she divined my distress, and, when she divined that it was chiefly for her, she set herself to console and reassure me. She told me that this was something every one here expected, in coming willingly or unwillingly before the public; and that I must not think of it at all, for certainly no one else would think twice of it. This, I found, was really so, for when I ventured to refer tentatively to some of these publications, I found that people, if they had read them, had altogether forgotten them; and that they were, with all the glare of print, of far less effect with our acquaintance than something said under the breath in a corner. I found that some of our friends had not known the effigies for ours which they had seen in the papers; others made a joke of the whole affair, as the Americans do with so many affairs, and said that they supposed the pictures were those of people who had been cured by some patent medicine, they looked so strong and handsome. This, I think, was a piece of Mr. Makely's humor in the beginning; but it had a general vogue long after the interviews and the illustrations were forgotten.

XXV

I LINGER a little upon these trivial matters because I shrink from what must follow. They were scarcely blots upon our happiness; rather they were motes in the sunshine which had no other cloud. It is true that I was always somewhat puzzled by a certain manner in Mrs. Gray, which certainly was from no unfriendliness for me; she could not have been more affectionate to me, after our engagement, if I had been really her own son; and it was not until after our common kindness had confirmed itself upon the new footing that I felt this perplexing qualification on it. I felt it first one day when I found her alone, and I talked long and freely to her of Eveleth, and opened to her my whole heart of joy in our love. At one point she casually asked me how soon we should expect to return from Altruria after our visit; and at first I did not understand.

"Of course," she explained, "you will want to see all your old friends, and so will Eveleth, for they will be her friends, too; but if you want me to go with you, as you say, you must let me know when I shall see New York again."

"Why," I said, "you will always be with us."

"Well, then," she pursued, with a smile, "when shall *you* come back?"

"Oh, never!" I answered. "No one ever leaves Altruria, if he can help it, unless he is sent on a mission."

She looked a little mystified, and I went on: "Of course, I was not officially authorized to visit the world outside, but I was permitted to do so, to satisfy a curiosity the priors thought useful; but I have now had quite enough of it, and I shall never leave home again."

"You won't come to live in America?"

"God forbid!" said I, and I am afraid I could not hide the horror that ran through me at the thought. "And when you once see our happy country, you could no more be persuaded to return to America than a disembodied spirit could be persuaded to return to the earth."

She was silent, and I asked: "But, surely, you understood this, Mrs. Gray?"

"No," she said, reluctantly. "Does Eveleth?"

"Why, certainly," I said. "We have talked it over a hundred times. Hasn't she—"

"I don't know," she returned, with a vague trouble in her voice and eyes. "Perhaps I haven't understood her exactly. Perhaps — but I shall be ready to do whatever you and she think best. I am an old woman, you know; and, you know, I was born here, and I should feel the change."

Her words conveyed to me a delicate reproach; I felt for the first time that, in my love of my own country, I had not considered her love of hers. It is said that the Icelanders are homesick when they leave their world of lava and snow; and I ought to have remembered that an American might have some such tenderness for his atrocious conditions, if he were exiled from them forever. I suppose it was the large and wide mind of Eveleth, with its openness to a knowledge and appreciation of better things, that had suffered me to forget this. She seemed always so eager to see

112

Altruria, she imagined it so fully, so lovingly, that I had ceased to think of her as an alien; she seemed one of us, by birth as well as by affinity.

Yet now the words of her mother, and the light they threw upon the situation, gave me pause. I began to ask myself questions I was impatient to ask Eveleth, so that there should be no longer any shadow of misgiving in my breast; and yet I found myself dreading to ask them, lest by some perverse juggle I had mistaken our perfect sympathy for a perfect understanding.

XXVI

Like all cowards who wait a happy moment for the duty that should not be suffered to wait at all, I was destined to have the affair challenge me, instead of seizing the advantage of it that instant frankness would have given me. Shall I confess that I let several days go by, and still had not spoken to Eveleth, when, at the end of a long evening—the last long evening we passed together—she said:

"What would you like to have me do with this house while we are gone?"

"Do with this house?" I echoed; and I felt as if I were standing on the edge of an abyss.

"Yes; shall we let it, or sell it—or what? Or give it away?" I drew a little breath at this; perhaps we had not misunderstood each other, after all. She went on: "Of course, I have a peculiar feeling about it, so that I wouldn't like to get it ready and let it furnished, in the ordinary way. I would rather lend it to some one, if I could be sure of any one who would appreciate it; but I can't. Not one. And it's very much the same when one comes to think about selling it. Yes, I should like to give it away for some good purpose, if there is any in this wretched state of things. What do you say, Aristide?"

She always used the French form of my name, because she said it sounded ridiculous in English, for a white man, though I told her that the English was nearer the Greek in sound.

114

" By all means, give it away," I said. " Give it for
some public purpose. That will at least be better than
any private purpose, and put it somehow in the control
of the State, beyond the reach of individuals or cor-
porations. Why not make it the foundation of a free
school for the study of the Altrurian polity?"

She laughed at this, as if she thought I must be
joking. " It would be droll, wouldn't it, to have Tammany appointees teaching Altrurianism?" Then she
said, after a moment of reflection: " Why not? It
needn't be in the hands of Tammany. It could be in
the hands of the United States; I will ask my lawyer
if it couldn't; and I will endow it with money enough
to support the school handsomely. Aristide, you have
hit it!"

I began: " You can give *all* your money to it, my
dear—" But I stopped at the bewildered look she
turned on me.

" All?" she repeated. " But what should we have
to live on, then?"

" We shall need no money to live on in Altruria,"
I answered.

" Oh, in Altruria! But when we come back to New
York?"

It was an agonizing moment, and I felt that shut-
ting of the heart which blinds the eyes and makes the
brain reel. " Eveleth," I gasped, " did you expect to
return to New York?"

" Why, certainly!" she cried. " Not at once, of
course. But after you had seen your friends, and
made a good, long visit— Why, surely, Aristide, you
don't understand that I— You didn't mean to *live* in
'Altruria?"

" Ah!" I answered. " Where else could I live?
Did you think for an instant that I could live in such

a land as this?" I saw that she was hurt, and I hastened to say: "I know that it is the best part of the world outside of Altruria, but, oh, my dear, you cannot imagine how horrible the notion of living here seems to me. Forgive me. I am going from bad to worse. I don't mean to wound you. After all, it is your country, and you must love it. But, indeed, I could not think of living here. I could not take the burden of its wilful misery on my soul. I must live in Altruria, and you, when you have once seen my country, *our* country, will never consent to live in any other."

"Yes," she said, "I know it must be very beautiful; but I hadn't supposed—and yet I ought—"

"No, dearest, no! It was I who was to blame, for not being clearer from the first. But that is the way with us. We can't imagine any people willing to live anywhere else when once they have seen Altruria; and I have told you so much of it, and we have talked of it together so often, that I must have forgotten you had not actually known it. But listen, Eveleth. We will agree to this: After we have been a year in Altruria, if you wish to return to America I will come back and live with you here."

"No, indeed!" she answered, generously. "If you are to be my husband," and here she began with the solemn words of the Bible, so beautiful in their quaint English, "'whither thou goest, I will go, and I will not return from following after thee. Thy country shall be my country, and thy God my God.'"

I caught her to my heart, in a rapture of tenderness, and the evening that had begun for us so forbiddingly ended in a happiness such as not even our love had known before. I insisted upon the conditions I had made, as to our future home, and she agreed to them gayly at last, as a sort of reparation which I might make my conscience, if I liked, for tearing her from a country which she had willingly lived out of for the far greater part of the last five years.

But when we met again I could see that she had been thinking seriously.

" I won't give the house absolutely away," she said. " I will keep the deed of it myself, but I will establish that sort of school of Altrurian doctrine in it, and I will endow it, and when we come back here, for our experimental sojourn, after we've been in Altruria a year, we'll take up our quarters in it—I won't give the whole house to the school — and we will lecture on the later phases of Altrurian life to the pupils. How will that do?"

She put her arms around my neck, and I said that it would do admirably; but I had a certain sinking of the heart, for I saw how hard it was even for Eveleth to part with her property.

" I'll endow it," she went on, " and I'll leave the rest of my money at interest here; unless you think that some Altrurian securities—"

" No; there are no such things!" I cried.

" That was what I thought," she returned; " and as it will cost us nothing while we are in Altruria, the interest will be something very handsome by the time we get back, even in United States bonds."

" Something handsome!" I cried. " But, Eveleth, haven't I heard you say yourself that the growth of interest from dead money was like—"

" Oh yes; that!" she returned. " But you know you have to take it. You can't let the money lie idle: that would be ridiculous; and then, with the good purpose we have in view, it is our *duty* to take the interest. How should we keep up the school, and pay the teachers, and everything?"

I saw that she had forgotten the great sum of the principal, or that, through lifelong training and association, it was so sacred to her that she did not even dream of touching it. I was silent, and she thought that I was persuaded.

"You are perfectly right in theory, dear, and I feel just as you do about such things; I'm sure I've suffered enough from them; but if we didn't take interest for your money, what should we have to live on?"

"Not *my* money, Eveleth!" I entreated. "Don't say *my* money!"

"But whatever is mine is yours," she returned, with a wounded air.

"Not your money; but I hope you will soon have none. We should need no money to live on in Altruria. Our share of the daily work of all will amply suffice for our daily bread and shelter."

"In Altruria, yes. But how about America? And you have promised to come back here in a year, you know. Ladies and gentlemen can't share in the daily toil here, even if they could get the toil, and, where there are so many out of work, it isn't probable they could."

She dropped upon my knee as she spoke, laughing, and put her hand under my chin, to lift my fallen face.

"Now you mustn't be a goose, Aristide, even if you *are* an angel! Now listen. You *know,* don't you, that I hate money just as badly as you?"

"You have made me think so, Eveleth," I answered.

"I hate it and loathe it. I think it's the source of all the sin and misery in the world; but you can't get rid of it at a blow. For if you gave it away you might do more harm than good with it."

118

" You could destroy it," I said.

" Not unless you were a crank," she returned.
" And that brings me just to the point. I know that
I'm doing a very queer thing to get married, when we
know so little, really, about you," and she accented
this confession with a laugh that was also a kiss. " But
I want to show people that we are just as practical as
anybody; and if they can know that I have left my
money in United States bonds, they'll respect us, no
matter what I do with the interest. Don't you see?
We can come back, and preach and teach Altrurianism,
and as long as we pay our way nobody will have a right
to say a word. Why, Tolstoy himself doesn't destroy
his money, though he wants other people to do it. His
wife keeps it, and supports the family. You *have* to
do it."

" He doesn't do it willingly."

" No. And *we* won't. And after a while — after
we've got back, and compared Altruria and America
from practical experience, if we decide to go and live
there altogether, I will let you do what you please with
the hateful money. I suppose we couldn't take it there
with us?"

" No more than you could take it to heaven with
you," I answered, solemnly; but she would not let me
be altogether serious about it.

" Well, in either case we could get on without it,
though we certainly could not get on without it here.
Why, Aristide, it is essential to the influence we shall
try to exert for Altrurianism; for if we came back
here and preached the true life without any money to
back us, no one would pay any attention to us. But
if we have a good house waiting for us, and are able
to entertain nicely, we can attract the best people, and
—and—really do some good."

XXVII

I ROSE in a distress which I could not hide. "Oh, Eveleth, Eveleth!" I cried. "You are like all the rest, poor child! You are the creature of your environment, as we all are. You cannot escape what you have been. It may be that I was wrong to wish or expect you to cast your lot with me in Altruria, at once and forever. It may be that it is my duty to return here with you after a time, not only to let you see that Altruria is best, but to end my days in this unhappy land, preaching and teaching Altrurianism; but we must not come as prophets to the comfortable people, and entertain nicely. If we are to renew the evangel, it must be in the life and the spirit of the First Altrurian: we must come poor to the poor; we must not try to win any one, save through his heart and conscience; we must be as simple and humble as the least of those that Christ bade follow Him. Eveleth, perhaps you have made a mistake. I love you too much to wish you to suffer even for your good. Yes, I am so weak as that. I did not think that this would be the sacrifice for you that it seems, and I will not ask it of you. I am sorry that we have not understood each other, as I supposed we had. I could never become an American; perhaps you could never become an Altrurian. Think of it, dearest. Think well of it, before you take the step which you cannot recede from. I hold you to no promise; I love you so dearly that I cannot let you hold yourself. But you must choose between me and your money—no, not me—but between love and your money. You cannot keep both."

She had stood listening to me; now she cast herself on my heart and stopped my words with an impassioned kiss. "Then there is no choice for me. My choice is made, once for all." She set her hands against my breast and pushed me from her. "Go now; but come again to-morrow. I want to think it all over again. Not that I have any doubt, but because you wish it—you wish it, don't you?—and because I will not let you ever think I acted upon an impulse, and that I regretted it."

"That is right, Eveleth. That is like *you*," I said, and I took her into my arms for good-night.

The next day I came for her decision, or rather for her confirmation of it. The man who opened the door to me met me with a look of concern and embarrassment. He said Mrs. Strange was not at all well, and had told him he was to give me the letter he handed me. I asked, in taking it, if I could see Mrs. Gray, and he answered that Mrs. Gray had not been down yet, but he would go and see. I was impatient to read my letter, and I made I know not what vague reply, and I found myself, I know not how, on the pavement, with the letter open in my hand. It began abruptly without date or address:

"*You will believe that I have not slept, when you read this.*

"*I have thought it all over again, as you wished, and it is all over between us.*

"*I am what you said, the creature of my environment. I cannot detach myself from it; I cannot escape from what I have been.*

"*I am writing this with a strange coldness, like the*
121

chill of death, in my very soul. I do not ask you to forgive me; I have your forgiveness already. Do not forget me; that is what I ask. Remember me as the unhappy woman who was not equal to her chance when heaven was opened to her, who could not choose the best when the best came to her.

"There is no use writing; if I kept on forever, it would always be the same cry of shame, of love.

"Eveleth Strange."

I reeled as I read the lines. The street seemed to weave itself into a circle around me. But I knew that I was not dreaming, that this was no delirium of my sleep.

It was three days ago, and I have not tried to see her again. I have written her a line, to say that I shall not forget her, and to take the blame upon myself. I expected the impossible of her.

I have yet two days before me until the steamer sails; we were to have sailed together, and now I shall sail alone.

I will try to leave it all behind me forever; but while I linger out these last long hours here I must think and I must doubt.

Was she, then, the *poseuse* that they said? Had she really no heart in our love? Was it only a pretty drama she was playing, and were those generous motives, those lofty principles which seemed to actuate her, the poetical qualities of the play, the graces of her pose? I cannot believe it. I believe that she was truly what she seemed, for she had been that even before she met me. I believe that she was pure and lofty in soul as she appeared; but that her life was warped to such a form by the false conditions of this sad world that, when she came to look at herself again, after she

122

had been confronted with the sacrifice before her, she feared that she could not make it without in a manner ceasing to be.

She—

But I shall soon see you again; and, until then, farewell.

END OF PART I

PART SECOND

I

I COULD hardly have believed, my dear Dorothea, that I should be so late in writing to you from Altruria, but you can easily believe that I am thoroughly ashamed of myself for my neglect. It is not for want of thinking of you, or talking of you, that I have seemed so much more ungrateful than I am. My husband and I seldom have any serious talk which doesn't somehow come round to you. He admires you and likes you as much as I do, and he does his best, poor man, to understand you; but his not understanding you is only a part of his general failure to understand how any American can be kind and good in conditions which he considers so abominable as those of the capitalistic world. He is not nearly so severe on us as he used to be at times when he was among us. When the other Altrurians are discussing us he often puts in a reason for us against their logic; and I think he has really forgotten, a good deal, how bad things are with us, or else finds his own memory of them incredible. But his experience of the world outside his own country has taught him how to temper the passion of the Altrurians for justice with a tolerance of the unjust; and when they bring him to book on his own report of us he tries to explain us away, and show how we are not so bad as we ought to be.

For weeks after we came to Altruria I was so unhistorically blest that if I had been disposed to give you a full account of myself I should have had no events to hang the narrative on. Life here is so subjective (if you don't know what that is, you poor dear, you must get Mr. Twelvemough to explain) that there is usually nothing like news in it, and I always feel that the difference between Altruria and America is so immense that it is altogether beyond me to describe it. But now we have had some occurrences recently, quite in the American sense, and these have furnished me with an incentive as well as opportunity to send you a letter. Do you remember how, one evening after dinner, in New York, you and I besieged my husband and tried to make him tell us why Altruria was so isolated from the rest of the world, and why such a great and enlightened continent should keep itself apart? I see still his look of horror when Mr. Makely suggested that the United States should send an expedition and "open" Altruria, as Commodore Perry "opened" Japan in 1850, and try to enter into commercial relations with it. The best he could do was to say what always seemed so incredible, and keep on assuring us that Altruria wished for no sort of public relations with Europe or America, but was very willing to depend for an indefinite time for its communication with those regions on vessels putting into its ports from stress of one kind or other, or castaway on its coasts. They are mostly trading-ships or whalers, and they come a great deal oftener than you suppose; you do not hear of them afterwards, because their crews are poor, ignorant people, whose stories of their adventures are always distrusted, and who know they would be laughed at if they told the stories they could of a country like Altruria. My husband himself took one of their vessels on her home voyage when he came to us, catching the Australasian steamer at New Zealand; and now I am writing you by the same sort of opportunity. I shall have time

enough to write you a longer letter than you will care
to read; the ship does not sail for a week yet, because
it is so hard to get her crew together.

Now that I have actually made a beginning, my
mind goes back so strongly to that terrible night when
I came to you after Aristides (I always use the English form of his name now) left New York that I
seem to be living the tragedy over again, and this
happiness of mine here is like a dream which I cannot trust. It was not all tragedy, though, and I remember how funny Mr. Makely was, trying to keep
his face straight when the whole truth had to come
out, and I confessed that I had expected, without
really knowing it myself, that Aristides would dis-
regard that wicked note I had written him and come
and make me marry him, not against my will, but
against my word. Of course I didn't put it in just
that way, but in a way to let you both guess it. The
first glimmering of hope that I had was when Mr.
Makely said, " Then, when a woman tells a man that
all is over between them forever, she means that she
would like to discuss the business with him ?" I was
old enough to be ashamed, but it seemed to me that you
and I had gone back in that awful moment and were
two girls together, just as we used to be at school. I
was proud of the way you stood up for me, because I
thought that if you could tolerate me after what I had
confessed I could not be quite a fool. I knew that I
deserved at least some pity, and though I laughed with
Mr. Makely, I was glad of your indignation with him,
and of your faith in Aristides. When it came to the
question of what I should do, I don't know which of
you I owed the most to. It was a kind of comfort to
have Mr. Makely acknowledge that though he regarded
Aristides as a myth, still he believed that he was a

thoroughly *good* myth, and couldn't tell a lie if he wanted to; and I loved you, and shall love you more than any one else but him, for saying that Aristides was the most real man you had ever met, and that if everything he said was untrue you would trust him to the end of the world.

But, Dolly, it wasn't all comedy, any more than it was all tragedy, and when you and I had laughed and cried ourselves to the point where there was nothing for me to do but to take the next boat for Liverpool, and Mr. Makely had agreed to look after the tickets and cable Aristides that I was coming, there was still my poor, dear mother to deal with. There is no use trying to conceal from you that she was always opposed to my husband. She thought there was something uncanny about him, though she felt as we did that there was nothing uncanny *in* him; but a man who pretended to come from a country where there was no riches and no poverty could not be trusted with any woman's happiness; and though she could not help loving him, she thought I ought to tear him out of my heart, and if I could not do that I ought to have myself shut up in an asylum. We had a dreadful time when I told her what I had decided to do, and I was almost frantic. At last, when she saw that I was determined to follow him, she yielded, not because she was convinced, but because she could not give me up; I wouldn't have let her if she could. I believe that the only thing which reconciled her was that you and Mr. Makely believed in him, and thought I had better do what I wanted to, if nothing could keep me from it. I shall never, never forget Mr. Makely's goodness in coming to talk with her, and how skilfully he managed, without committing himself to Altruria, to declare his faith in my Altrurian. Even then she was troubled about what she thought the indelicacy of my behavior in following him across the sea, and she had all sorts of doubts as to how he would receive me when we met in Liverpool. It wasn't very reasonable of me to say that if he cast me off I should still love him more than any other human being, and his censure would be more precious to me than the praise of the rest of the world.

I suppose I hardly knew what I was saying, but when once I had yielded to my love for him there was nothing else in life. I could not have left my mother behind, but in her opposition to me she seemed like an enemy, and I should somehow have *forced* her to go if she had not yielded. When she did yield, she yielded with her whole heart and soul, and so far from hindering me in my preparations for the voyage, I do not believe I could have got off without her. She thought about everything, and it was her idea to leave my business affairs entirely in Mr. Makely's hands, and to trust the future for the final disposition of my property. I did not care for it myself; I hated it, because it was that which had stood between me and Aristides; but she foresaw that if by any wild impossibility he should reject me when we met, I should need it for the life I must go back to in New York. She behaved like a martyr as well as a heroine, for till we reached Altruria she was a continual sacrifice to me. She stubbornly doubted the whole affair, but now I must do her the justice to say that she has been convinced by the fact. The best she can say of it is that it is like the world of her girlhood; and she has gone back to the simple life here from the artificial life in New York, with the joy of a child. She works the whole day, and she would play if she had ever learned how. She is a better Altrurian than I am; if there could be a bigoted Altrurian my mother would be one.

II

I SENT you a short letter from Liverpool, saying that
by the unprecedented delays of the *Urània,* which I
had taken because it was the swiftest boat of the Nep-
tune line, we had failed to pass the old, ten-day, single-
screw Galaxy liner which Aristides had sailed in. I
had only time for a word to you; but a million words
could not have told the agonies I suffered, and when
I overtook him on board the Orient Pacific steamer
at Plymouth, where she touched, I could just scribble
off the cable sent Mr. Makely before our steamer put
off again. I am afraid you did not find my cable very
expressive, but I was glad that I did not try to say
more, for if I had tried I should simply have gibbered,
at a shilling a gibber. I expected to make amends by
a whole volume of letters, and I did post a dozen under
one cover from Colombo. If they never reached you
I am very sorry, for now it is impossible to take up the
threads of that time and weave them into any sort of
connected pattern. You will have to let me off with
saying that Aristides was everything that I believed
he would be and was never really afraid he might not
be. From the moment we caught sight of each other at
Plymouth, he at the rail of the steamer and I on the
deck of the tender, we were as completely one as we
are now. I never could tell how I got aboard to him;
whether he came down and brought me, or whether I was
simply rapt through the air to his side. It would have
been embarrassing if we had not treated the situation

frankly; but such odd things happen among the English going out to their different colonies that our marriage, by a missionary returning to his station, was not even a nine days' wonder with our fellow-passengers.

We were a good deal more than nine days on the steamer before we could get a vessel that would take us on to Altruria; but we overhauled a ship going there for provisions at last, and we were all put off on her, bag and baggage, with three cheers from the friends we were leaving; I think they thought we were going to some of the British islands that the Pacific is full of. I had been thankful from the first that I had not brought a maid, knowing the Altrurian prejudice against hireling service, but I never was so glad as I was when we got aboard that vessel, for when the captain's wife, who was with him, found that I had no one to look after me, she looked after me herself, just for the fun of it, she said; but *I* knew it was the love of it. It was a sort of general trading-ship, stopping at the different islands in the South Seas, and had been a year out from home, where the kind woman had left her little ones; she cried over their photographs to me. Her husband had been in Altruria before, and he and Aristides were old acquaintances and met like brothers; some of the crew knew him, too, and the captain relaxed discipline so far as to let us shake hands with the second-mate as the men's representative.

I needn't dwell on the incidents of our home-coming —for that was what it seemed for my mother and me as well as for my husband—but I must give you one detail of our reception, for I still think it almost the prettiest thing that has happened to us among the millions of pretty things. Aristides had written home of our engagement, and he was expected with his American wife; and before we came to anchor the captain ran up the Emissary's signal, which my husband gave him, and then three boats left the shore and pulled rapidly out to us. As they came nearer I saw the first Altrurian costumes in the lovely colors that the people wear here, and that make a group of them look like a flower-bed; and then I saw that the boats were banked with flowers along the gunwales from stem to stern, and that they were each not *manned,* but *girled* by six rowers, who pulled as true a stroke as I ever saw in our boat-races. When they caught sight of us, leaning over the side, and Aristides lifted his hat and waved it to them, they all stood their oars upright, and burst into a kind of welcome song: I had been dreading one of those stupid, banging salutes of ten or twenty guns, and you can imagine what a relief it was. They were great, splendid creatures, as tall as our millionaires' tallest daughters, and as strong-looking as any of our college-girl athletes; and when we got down over the ship's side, and Aristides said a few words of introduction for my mother and me, as we stepped into the largest of the boats, I thought they would crush me, catching me in their strong, brown arms, and kissing me on each cheek; they never kiss on the mouth in Altruria. The girls in the other boats kissed their hands to mother and me, and shouted to Aristides, and then, when our boat set out for the shore, they got on each side of us and sang song after song as they pulled even stroke with our crew. Half-way, we met three other boats, really *manned,* these ones, and going out to get our baggage, and then you ought to have heard the shouting and laughing, that ended in more singing, when the young fellows' voices mixed with the girls, till they were lost in the welcome that came off to us from the crowded quay, where I should have thought half Altruria had gathered to receive us.

134

I was afraid it was going to be too much for my
mother, but she stood it bravely; and almost at a glance
people began to take her into consideration, and she
was delivered over to two young married ladies, who
saw that she was made comfortable, the first of any,
in the pretty Regionic guest-house where they put us.

I wish I could give you a notion of that guest-house,
with its cool, quiet rooms, and its lawned and gardened
enclosure, and a little fountain purring away among the
flowers! But what astonished me was that there were
no sort of carriages, or wheeled conveyances, which,
after our escort from the ship, I thought might very
well have met the returning Emissary and his wife.
They made my mother get into a litter, with soft cush-
ions and with lilac curtains blowing round it, and six
girls carried her up to the house; but they seemed not
to imagine my not walking, and, in fact, I could hardly have imagined it myself, after the first moment of
queerness. That walk was full of such rich experience
for every one of the senses that I would not have
missed a step of it; but as soon as I could get Aristides
alone I asked him about horses, and he said that though
horses were still used in farm work, not a horse was
allowed in any city or village of Altruria, because of
their filthiness. As for public vehicles, they used to
have electric trolleys; in the year that he had been
absent they had substituted electric motors; but these
were not running, because it was a holiday on which
we had happened to arrive.

There was another incident of my first day which
I think will amuse you, knowing how I have always
shrunk from any sort of public appearances. When
Aristides went to make his report to the people assem-
bled in a sort of convention, I had to go too, and take
part in the proceedings; for women are on an entire

equality with the men here, and people would be shocked if husband and wife were separated in their public life. They did not spare me a single thing. Where Aristides was not very clear, or rather not full enough, in describing America, I was called on to supplement, and I had to make several speeches. Of course, as I spoke in English, he had to put it into Altrurian for me, and it made the greatest excitement. The Altrurians are very lively people, and as full of the desire to hear some new things as Paul said the men of Athens were. At times they were in a perfect gale of laughter at what we told them about America. Afterwards some of the women confessed to me that they liked to hear us speaking English together; it sounded like the whistling of birds or the shrilling of locusts. But they were perfectly kind, and though they laughed it was clear that they laughed at what we were saying, and never at us, or at least never at *me*.

Of course there was the greatest curiosity to know what Aristides' wife looked like, as well as sounded like; he had written out about our engagement before I broke it; and my clothes were of as much interest as myself, or more. You know how I had purposely left my latest Paris things behind, so as to come as simply as possible to the simple life of Altruria, but still with my big leg-of-mutton sleeves, and my picture-hat, and my pinched waist, I felt perfectly grotesque, and I have no doubt I looked it. They had never seen a lady from the capitalistic world before, but only now and then a whaling-captain's wife who had come ashore; and I knew they were burning to examine my smart clothes down to the last button and bit of braid. I had on the short skirts of last year, and I could feel ten thousand eyes fastened on my high-heeled boots, which you know *I* never went to extremes in. I confess my face burned a little, to realize what a scarecrow I must look, when I glanced round at those Altrurian women, whose pretty, classic fashions made the whole place like a field of lilacs and irises, and knew that they were as comfortable as they were beautiful. Do you remember some of the descriptions of the undergraduate maidens in the " Princess "—I know you had it at school—where they are sitting in the palace halls together? The effect was something like that.

You may be sure that I got out of my things as soon as I could borrow an Altrurian costume, and now my Paris confections are already hung up for monuments, as Richard III. says, in the Capitalistic Museum, where people from the outlying Regions may come and study them as object - lessons in what not to wear. (You remember what you said Aristides told you, when he spoke that day at the mountains, about the Regions that Altruria is divided into? This is the Maritime Region, and the city where we are living for the present is the capital.) You may think this was rather hard on me, and at first it did seem pretty intimate, having my things in a long glass case, and it gave me a shock to see them, as if it had been my ghost, whenever I passed them. But the fact is I was more ashamed than hurt — they were so ugly and stupid and useless. I could have borne my Paris dress and my picture-hat if it had not been for those ridiculous high - heeled, pointed - toe shoes, which the Curatress had stood at the bottom of the skirts. They looked the most frantic things you can imagine, and the mere sight of them made my poor feet *ache* in the beautiful sandals I am wearing now; when once you have put on sandals you say good-bye and good-riddance to shoes. In a single month my feet have grown almost a tenth as large again as they were, and my friends here encourage me to believe that they will yet measure nearly the classic size, though, as you know, I am not in my first youth and can't expect them to do miracles.

I had to leave off abruptly at the last page because Aristides had come in with a piece of news that took my mind off everything else. I am afraid you are not going to get this letter even at the late date I had set for its reaching you, my dear. It seems that there has been a sort of mutiny among the crew of our trader, which was to sail next week, and now there is no telling when she will sail. Ever since she came the men have been allowed their liberty, as they call it, by watches, but the last watch came ashore this week before another watch had returned to the ship, and now not one of the sailors will go back. They had been exploring the country by turns, at their leisure, it seems, and their excuse is that they like Altruria better than America, which they say they wish never to see again.

You know (though I didn't, till Aristides explained to me) that in any European country the captain in such a case would go to his consul, and the consul would go to the police, and the police would run the men down and send them back to the ship in irons as deserters, or put them in jail till the captain was ready to sail, and then deliver them up to him. But it seems that there is no law in Altruria to do anything of the kind; the only law here that would touch the case is one which obliges any citizen to appear and answer the complaint of any other citizen before the Justiciary Assembly. A citizen cannot be imprisoned for anything but the rarest offence, like killing a person in a fit of passion; and as to seizing upon men who are guilty of nothing worse than wanting to be left to the pursuit of happiness, as all the Altrurians are, there is no statute and no usage for it. Aristides says that the only thing which can be done is to ask the captain and the men to come to the Assembly and each state his case. The Altrurians are not anxious to have the men stay, not merely because they are coarse, rude, or vicious, but because they think they ought to go home and tell the Americans what they have seen and heard here, and try and get them to found an Altrurian Commonwealth of their own. Still they will not compel them to go, and the magistrates do not wish to rouse any sort of sentiment against them. They feel that the men are standing on their natural rights, which they could not abdicate if they would. I know this will appear perfectly ridiculous to Mr. Makely, and I confess myself that there seems something binding in a contract which ought to act on the men's consciences, at least.

III

WELL, my dear Dorothea, the hearing before the Assembly is over, and it has left us just where it found us, as far as the departure of our trader is concerned.

How I wish you could have been there! The hearing lasted three days, and I would not have missed a minute of it. As it was, I did not miss a syllable, and it was so deeply printed on my mind that I believe I could repeat it word for word if I had to. But, in the first place, I must try and realize the scene to you. I was once summoned as a witness in one of our courts, you remember, and I have never forgotten the horror of it: the hot, dirty room, with its foul air, the brutal spectators, the policemen stationed among them to keep them in order, the lawyers with the plaintiff and defendant seated all at one table, the uncouth abruptness of the clerks and janitors, or whatever, the undignified magistrate, who looked as if his lunch had made him drowsy, and who seemed half asleep, as he slouched in his arm-chair behind his desk. Instead of such a setting as this, you must imagine a vast marble amphitheatre, larger than the Metropolitan Opera, by three or four times, all the gradines overflowing (that is the word for the "liquefaction of the clothes" which poured over them), and looking like those Bermudan waters where the colors of the rainbow seem dropped around the coast. On the platform, or stage, sat the Presidents of the Assembly, and on a tier of seats behind and above them, the national Magistrates, who, as this is the cap-

ital of the republic for the time being, had decided to
be present at the hearing, because they thought the case
so very important. In the hollow space, just below
(like that where you remember the Chorus stood in
that Greek play which we saw at Harvard ages ago),
were the captain and the first-mate on one hand, and
the seamen on the other; the second-mate, our particular
friend, was not there because he never goes ashore anywhere, and had chosen to remain with the black cook in
charge of the ship. The captain's wife would rather
have stayed with them, but I persuaded her to come to
us for the days of the hearing, because the captain had
somehow thought we were opposed to him, and because
I thought she ought to be there to encourage him by her
presence. She sat next to me, in a hat which I wish
you could have seen, Dolly, and a dress which would
have set your teeth on edge; but inside of them I knew
she was one of the best souls in the world, and I loved
her the more for being the sight she was among those
wonderful Altrurian women.

The weather was perfect, as it nearly always is at
this time of year—warm, yet fresh, with a sky of that
"bleu impossible" of the Riviera on the clearest day.
Some people had parasols, but they put them down as
soon as the hearing began, and everybody could see perfectly. You would have thought they could not hear
so well, but a sort of immense sounding-plane was
curved behind the stage, so that not a word of the testimony on either side was lost to me in English. The
Altrurian translation was given the second day of the
hearing through a megaphone, as different in tone from
the thing that the man in the Grand Central Station
bellows the trains through as the *vox-humana* stop of
an organ is different from the fog-horn of a light-house.
The captain's wife was bashful, in her odd American

dress, but we had got seats near the tribune, rather out of sight, and there was nothing to hinder our hearing, like the *frou-frou* of stiff silks or starched skirts (which I am afraid we poor things in America like to make when we move) from the soft, filmy tissues that the Altrurian women wear; but I must confess that there was a good deal of whispering while the captain and the men were telling their stories. But no one except the interpreters, who were taking their testimony down in short-hand, to be translated into Altrurian and read at the subsequent hearing, could understand what they were saying, and so nobody was disturbed by the murmurs. The whispering was mostly near me, where I sat with the captain's wife, for everybody I knew got as close as they could and studied my face when they thought anything important or significant had been said. They are very quick at reading faces here; in fact, a great deal of the conversation is carried on in that way, or with the visible speech; and my Altrurian friends knew almost as well as I did when the speakers came to an interesting point. It was rather embarrassing for me, though, with the poor captain's wife at my side, to tell them, in my broken Altrurian, what the men were accusing the captain of.

I talk of the men, but it was really only one of them who at first, by their common consent, spoke for the rest. He was a middle-aged Yankee, and almost the only born American among them, for you know that our sailors, nowadays, are of every nationality under the sun — Portuguese, Norwegians, Greeks, Italians, Kanucks, and Kanakas, and even Cape Cod Indians. He said he guessed his story was the story of most sailors, and he had followed the sea his whole life. His story was dreadful, and I tried to persuade the captain's wife not to come to the hearing the next day,

when it was to be read in Altrurian; but she would
come. I was afraid she would be overwhelmed by the
public compassion, and would not know what to do;
for when something awful that the sailor had said
against the captain was translated the women all about
us cooed their sympathy with her, and pressed her hand
if they could, or patted her on the shoulder, to show
how much they pitied her. In Altruria they pity the
friends of those who have done wrong, and sometimes
even the wrong-doers themselves; and it is quite a luxury, for there is so little wrong-doing here: I tell them
that in America they would have as much pitying to
do as they could possibly ask. After the hearing that
day my friends, who were of a good many different
Refectories, as we call them here, wanted her to go and
lunch with them; but I got her quietly home with me,
and after she had had something to eat I made her lie
down awhile.

You won't care to have me go fully into the affair.
The sailors' spokesman told how he had been born on a
farm, where he had shared the family drudgery and
poverty till he grew old enough to run away. He
meant to go to sea, but he went first to a factory town
and worked three or four years in the mills. He never
went back to the farm, but he sent a little money
now and then to his mother; and he stayed on till he
got into trouble. He did not say just what kind of
trouble, but I fancied it was some sort of love-trouble;
he blamed himself for it; and when he left that town
to get away from the thought of it, as much as anything, and went to work in another town, he took to
drink; then, once, in a drunken spree, he found himself
in New York without knowing how. But it was in
what he called a sailors' boarding-house, and one morning, after he had been drinking overnight " with a very

pleasant gentleman," he found himself in the forecastle of a ship bound for Holland, and when the mate came and cursed him up and cursed him out he found himself in the foretop. I give it partly in his own language, because I cannot help it; and I only wish I could give it wholly in his language; it was so graphic and so full of queer Yankee humor. From that time on, he said, he had followed the sea; and at sea he was always a good temperance man, but Altruria was the only place he had ever kept sober ashore. He guessed that was partly because there was nothing to drink but unfermented grape-juice, and partly because there was nobody to drink with; anyhow, he had not had a drop here. Everywhere else, as soon as he left his ship, he made for a sailors' boarding-house, and then he did not know much till he found himself aboard ship and bound for somewhere that he did not know of. He was always, he said, a stolen man, as much as a negro captured on the west coast of Africa and sold to a slaver; and, he said, it was a slave's life he led between drinks, whether it was a long time or short. He said he would ask his mates if it was very different with them, and when he turned to them they all shouted back, in their various kinds of foreign accents, No, it was just the same with them, every one. Then he said that was how he came to ship on our captain's vessel, and though they could not all say the same, they nodded confirmation as far as he was concerned.

The captain looked sheepish enough at this, but he looked sorrowful, too, as if he could have wished it had been different, and he asked the man if he had been abused since he came on board. Well, the man said, not unless you called tainted salt-horse and weevilly biscuit abuse; and then the captain sat down again, and I could feel his poor wife shrinking beside me. The man said that he was comparatively well off on the captain's ship, and the life was not half such a dog's life as he had led on other vessels; but it was such that when he got ashore here in Altruria, and saw how *white* people lived, people that *used* each other white, he made up his mind that he would never go back to any ship alive. He hated a ship so much that if he could go home to America as a first-class passenger on a Cunard liner, John D. Rockefeller would not have money enough to hire him to do it. He was going to stay in Altruria till he died, if they would let him, and he guessed they would, if what he had heard about them was true. He just wanted, he said, while we were about it, to have a few of his mates tell their experience, not so much on board the *Little Sally,* but on shore, and since they could remember; and one after another did get up and tell their miserable stories. They were like the stories you sometimes read in your paper over your coffee, or that you can hear any time you go into the congested districts in New York; but I assure you, my dear, they seemed to me perfectly incredible here, though I had known hundreds of such stories at home. As I realized their facts I forgot where I was; I felt that I was back again in that horror, where it sometimes seemed to me I had no right to be fed or clothed or warm or clean in the midst of the hunger and cold and nakedness and dirt, and where I could only reconcile myself to my comfort because I knew my discomfort would not help others' misery.

I can hardly tell how, but even the first day a sense of something terrible spread through that multitude of people, to whom the words themselves were mere empty sounds. The captain sat through it, with his head drooping, till his face was out of sight, and the tears ran silently down his wife's cheeks; and the women round me were somehow awed into silence. When the men ended, and there seemed to be no one else to say anything on that side, the captain jumped to his feet, with a sort of ferocious energy, and shouted out, "Are you all through, men?" and their spokesman answered, "Ay, ay, sir!" and then the captain flung back his grizzled hair and shook his fist towards the sailors. "And do you think I *wanted* to do it? Do you think I *liked* to do it? Do you think that if I hadn't been *afraid* my whole life long I would have had the *heart* to lead you the dog's life I know I've led you? I've been as poor as the poorest of you, and as low down as the lowest; I was born in the town poor-house, and I've been so afraid of the poor-house all my days that I hain't had, as you may say, a minute's peace. Ask my wife, there, what sort of a man I *am,* and whether I'm the man, *really* the man that's been hard and mean to you the way I know I been. It was because I was *afraid,* and because a coward is always hard and mean. I been afraid, ever since I could remember anything, of coming to want, and I was willing to see other men suffer so I could make sure that me and mine shouldn't suffer. That's the way we do at home, ain't it? That's in the day's work, ain't it? That's playing the game, ain't it, for everybody? You can't say it ain't." He stopped, and the men's spokesman called back, "Ay, ay, sir," as he had done before, and as I had often heard the men do when given an order on the ship.

The captain gave a kind of sobbing laugh, and went on in a lower tone. "Well, I know you ain't going back. I guess I didn't expect it much from the start, and I guess I'm not surprised." Then he lifted his head and shouted, "And do you suppose *I* want to go

146

back? Don't you suppose *I* would like to spend the rest of my days, too, among *white* people, people that *use* each other white, as you say, and where there ain't any want or, what's worse, *fear* of want? Men! There ain't a day, or an hour, or a minute, when I don't think how awful it is over there, where I got to be either some man's slave or some man's master, as much so as if it was down in the ship's articles. My wife ain't so, because she ain't been ashore here. I wouldn't let her; I was afraid to let her see what a white man's country really was, because I felt so weak about it myself, and I didn't want to put the trial on her, too. And do you know *why* we're going back, or want to go? I guess some of you know, but I want to tell these folks here so they'll understand, and I want you, Mr. Homos," he called to my husband, " to get it down straight. It's because we've got two little children over there, that we left with their grandmother when my wife come with me this voyage because she had lung difficulty and wanted to see whether she could get her health back. Nothing else on God's green earth could take me back to America, and I guess it couldn't my wife if she knew what Altruria was as well as I do. But when I went around here and saw how everything was, and remembered how it was at home, I just said, ' She'll stay on the ship.' Now, that's all I got to say, though I thought I had a lot more. I guess it 'll be enough for these folks, and they can judge between us." Then the captain sat down, and to make a long story short, the facts of the hearing were repeated in Altrurian the next day by megaphone, and when the translation was finished there was a general rush for the captain. He plainly expected to be lynched, and his wife screamed out, "Oh, don't hurt him! He isn't a bad man!" But it was only the Altrurian way with a guilty person: they

147

wanted to let him know how sorry they were for him, and since his sin had found him out how hopeful they were for his redemption. I had to explain it to the sailors as well as to the captain and his wife, but I don't believe any of them quite accepted the fact.

The third day of the hearing was for the rendering of the decision, first in Altrurian, and then in English. The verdict of the magistrates had to be confirmed by a standing vote of the people, and of course the women voted as well as the men. The decision was that the sailors should be absolutely free to go or stay, but they took into account the fact that it would be cruel to keep the captain and his wife away from their little ones, and the sailors might wish to consider this. If they still remained true to their love of Altruria they could find some means of returning.

When the translator came to this point their spokesman jumped to his feet and called out to the captain, "Will you *do* it?" "Do what?" he asked, getting slowly to his own feet. " Come back with us after you have seen the kids?" The captain shook his fist at the sailors; it seemed to be the only gesture he had with them. " Give me the *chance!* All I want is to see the children and bring them out with me to Altruria, and the old folks with them." " Will you *swear* it? Will you say, ' I hope I may find the kids dead and buried when I get home if I don't do it '?" " I'll take that oath, or any oath you want me to." " Shake hands on it, then."

The two men met in front of the tribunal and clasped hands there, and their reconciliation did not need translation. Such a roar of cheers went up! And then the whole assembly burst out in the national Altrurian anthem, "Brothers All." I wish you could have heard it! But when the terms of the agreement were explained, the cheering that had gone before was a mere whisper to what followed. One orator after another rose and praised the self-sacrifice of the sailors. I was the proudest when the last of them referred to Aristides and the reports which he had sent home from America, and said that without some such study as he had made of the American character they never could have understood such an act as they were now witnessing. Illogical and insensate as their system was, their character sometimes had a beauty, a sublimity which was not possible to Altrurians even, for it was performed in the face of risks and chances which their happy conditions relieved them from. At the same time, the orator wished his hearers to consider the essential immorality of the act. He said that civilized men had no right to take these risks and chances. The sailors were perhaps justified, in so far as they were homeless, wifeless, and childless men; but it must not be forgotten that their heroism was like the reckless generosity of savages.

The men have gone back to the ship, and she sails this afternoon. I have persuaded the captain to let his wife stay to lunch with me at our Refectory, where the ladies wish to bid her good-bye, and I am hurrying forward this letter so that she can take it on board with her this afternoon. She has promised to post it on the first Pacific steamer they meet, or if they do not meet any to send it forward to you with a special-delivery stamp as soon as they reach Boston. She will also forward by express an Altrurian costume, such as I am now wearing, sandals and all! Do put it on, Dolly, dear, for my sake, and realize what it is for once in your life to be a *free* woman.

Heaven knows when I shall have another chance of getting letters to you. But I shall live in hopes, and I shall set down my experiences here for your benefit, not perhaps as I meet them, but as I think of them, and you must not mind having a rather cluttered narrative. To-morrow we are setting off on our round of the capitals, where Aristides is to make a sort of public report to the people of the different Regions on the working of the capitalistic conditions as he observed them among us. But I don't expect to send you a continuous narrative of our adventures. Good-bye, dearest, with my mother's love, and my husband's as well as my own, to both of you; think of me as needing nothing but a glimpse of you to complete my happiness. How I should like to tell you fully about it! You *must* come to Altruria!

I came near letting this go without telling you of one curious incident of the affair between the captain and his men. Before the men returned to the ship they came with their spokesman to say good-bye to Aristides and me, and he remarked casually that it was just as well, maybe, to be going back, because, for one thing, they would know then whether it was real or not. I asked him what he meant, and he said, "Well, you know, some of the mates think it's a dream here, or it's too good to be true. As far forth as I go, I'd be willing to have it a dream that I didn't ever have to wake up from. It ain't any too good to be true for me. Anyway, I'm going to get back somehow, and give it another chance to be a fact." Wasn't that charming? It had a real touch of poetry in it, but it was prose that followed. I couldn't help asking him whether there had been nothing to mar the pleasure of their stay in Altruria, and he answered: "Well, I don't know as you could rightly say *mar;* it hadn't ought to have. You see, it was like this. You see, some of the mates wanted to

lay off and have a regular bange, but that don't seem to
be the idea here. After we had been ashore a day or
two they set us to work at different jobs, or wanted to.
The mates didn't take hold very lively, and some of 'em
didn't take hold a bit. But after that went on a couple
of days, there wa'n't any breakfast one morning, and
come noontime there wa'n't any dinner, and as far
forth as they could make out they had to go to bed
without supper. Then they called a halt, and tackled
one of your head men here that could speak some English. He didn't answer them right off the reel, but he
got out his English Testament and he read 'em a verse
that said, 'For even when we were with you this we
commanded you, that if any one would not work neither
should he eat.' That kind of fetched 'em, and after
that there wa'n't any sojerin', well not to speak of.
They saw he meant business. I guess it did more than
any one thing to make 'em think they wa'n't dreamin'.''

IV

You must not think, Dolly, from anything I have been telling you that the Altrurians are ever harsh. Sometimes they cannot realize how things really are with us, and how what seems grotesque and hideous to them seems charming and beautiful, or at least *chic,* to us. But they are wonderfully quick to see when they have hurt you the least, and in the little sacrifices I have made of my wardrobe to the cause of general knowledge there has not been the least urgence from them. When I now look at the things I used to wear, where they have been finally placed in the ethnological department of the Museum, along with the Esquimau kyaks and the Thlinkeet totems, they seem like things I wore in some prehistoric age—

"When wild in woods the noble savage ran."

Now, am *I* being unkind? Well, you mustn't mind me, Dolly. You must just say, " She *has* got it bad," and go on and learn as much about Altruria as you can from me. Some of the things were hard to get used to, and at first seemed quite impossible. For one thing, there was the matter of *service,* which is dishonorable with us, and honorable with the Altrurians: I was a long time getting to understand that, though I knew it perfectly well from hearing my husband talk about it in New York. I believe he once came pretty near offending you by asking why you did not do your own work, or something like that; he has confessed as much, and I could not wonder at you in your conditions. Why, when we first went to the guest-house, and the pretty young girls who brought in lunch sat down at table to eat it with us, I felt the indignation making me hot all over. You know how democratic I am, and I did not mind those great, splendid boat-girls hugging and kissing me, but I instinctively drew the line at cooks and waitresses. In New York, you know, I always tried to be kind to my servants, but as for letting one of them sit down in my presence, much less sit down at table with me, I never dreamed of such a thing in my most democratic moments. Luckily I drew the line subjectively here, and later I found that these young ladies were daughters of some of the most distinguished men and women on the continent, though you must not understand distinction as giving any sort of social primacy; that sort of thing is not allowed in Altruria. They had drawn lots with the girls in the Regionic school here, and were proud of having won the honor of waiting on us. Of course, I needn't say they were what we would have felt to be ladies anywhere, and their manners were exquisite, even to leaving us alone together as soon as we had finished luncheon. The meal itself was something I shall always remember for its delicious cooking of the different kinds of mushrooms which took the place of meat, and the wonderful salads, and the temperate and tropical fruits which we had for dessert.

They had to talk mostly with my husband, of course, and when they did talk to me it was through him. They were very intelligent about our world, much more than we are about Altruria, though, of course, it was by deduction from premises rather than specific information, and they wanted to ask a thousand questions; but they saw the joke of it, and laughed with us when Aristides put them off with a promise that if they would have a public meeting appointed we would appear and answer all the questions anybody could think of; we were not going to waste our answers on them the first day. He wanted them to let us go out and help wash the dishes, but they would not hear of it. I confess I was rather glad of that, for it seemed a lower depth to which I could not descend, even after eating with them. But they invited us out to look at the kitchen, after they had got it in order a little, and when we joined them there, whom should I see but my own dear old mother, with an apron up to her chin, wiping the glass and watching carefully through her dear old spectacles that she got everything bright! You know she was of a simpler day than ours, and when she was young she used to do her own work, and she and my father always washed the dishes together after they had company. I merely said, " *Well,* mother!" and she laughed and colored, and said she guessed she should like it in Altruria, for it took her back to the America she used to know.

I must mention things as they come into my head, and not in any regular order; there are too many of them. One thing is that I did not notice till afterwards that we had had no meat that first day at luncheon— the mushrooms were so delicious, and you know I never was much of a meat-eater. It was not till we began to make our present tour of the Regionic capitals, where Aristides has had to repeat his account of American civilization until I am sick as well as ashamed of America, that I first felt a kind of famine which I kept myself from recognizing as long as I could. Then I had to own to myself, long before I owned it to him,

that I was hungry for *meat*—for roast, for broiled, for
fried, for hashed. I did not actually tell him, but he
found it out, and I could not deny it, though I felt
such an ogre in it. He was terribly grieved, and blamed
himself for not having thought of it, and wished he had
got some canned meats from the trader before she left
the port. He was really in despair, for nobody since
the old capitalistic times had thought of killing sheep
or cattle for food; they have them for wool and milk
and butter; and of course when I looked at them in the
fields it did seem rather formidable. You are so used
to seeing them in the butchers' shops, ready for the
range, that you never think of what they have to *go
through* before that. But at last I managed to gasp
out, one day, "If I could only have a chicken!"
and he seemed to think that it could be managed. I
don't know how he made interest with the authorities,
or how the authorities prevailed on a farmer to part
with one of his precious pullets; but the thing was done
somehow, and two of the farmer's children brought it
to us at one of the guest-houses where we were staying,
and then fled howling. That was bad enough, but what
followed was worse. I went another day on mushrooms before I had the heart to say chicken again and
suggest that Aristides should get it killed and dressed.
The poor fellow did try, I believe, but we had to fall
back upon ourselves for the murderous deed, and—
Did you ever see a chicken have its head cut off, and
how hideously it behaves? It made us both wish we
were dead; and the sacrifice of that one pullet was quite
enough for me. We buried the poor thing under the
flowers of the guest-house garden, and I went back to
my mushrooms after a visit of contrition to the farmer
and many attempts to bring his children to forgiveness.
After all, the Altrurian mushrooms are wonderfully

nourishing, and they are in such variety that, what with other succulent vegetables and the endless range of fruits and nuts, one does not wish for meat—meat that one has killed one's self!

V

I wish you could be making tour of the Regionic capitals with us, Dolly! There are swift little one-rail electric expresses running daily from one capital to another, but these are used only when speed is required, and we are confessedly in no hurry: Aristides wanted me to see as much of the country as possible, and I am as eager as he. The old steam-roads of the capitalistic epoch have been disused for generations, and their beds are now the country roads, which are everywhere kept in beautiful repair. There are no horse vehicles (the electric motors are employed in the towns), though some people travel on horseback, but the favorite means of conveyance is by electric van, which any citizen may have on proof of his need of it; and it is comfortable beyond compare — mounted on easy springs, and curtained and cushioned like those gypsy vans we see in the country at home. Aristides drives himself, and sometimes we both get out and walk, for there is plenty of time.

I don't know whether I can make you understand how everything has tended to simplification here. They have disused the complicated facilities and conveniences of the capitalistic epoch, which we are so proud of, and have got back as close as possible to nature. People stay at home a great deal more than with us, though if any one likes to make a journey or to visit the capitals he is quite free to do it, and those who have some useful or beautiful object in view make

157

the sacrifice, as they feel it, to leave their villages every day and go to the nearest capital to carry on their studies or experiments. What we consider modern conveniences they would consider a superfluity of naughtiness for the most part. As *work* is the ideal, they do not believe in what we call labor-saving devices.

When we approach a village on our journey, one of the villagers, sometimes a young man, and sometimes a girl, comes out to meet us, and when we pass through they send some one with us on the way a little. The people have a perfect inspiration for hospitality: they not only know when to do and how much to do, but how little and when not at all. I can't remember that we have ever once been bored by those nice young things that welcomed us or speeded us on our way, and when we have stopped in a village they have shown a genius for leaving us alone, after the first welcome, that is beautiful. They are so regardful of our privacy, in fact, that if it had not been for Aristides, who explained their ideal to me, I should have felt neglected sometimes, and should have been shy of letting them know that we would like their company. But he understood it, and I must say that I have never enjoyed people and their ways so much. Their hospitality is a sort of compromise between that of the English houses where you are left free at certain houses to follow your own devices absolutely, and that Spanish splendor which assures you that the host's house is yours without meaning it. In fact, the guest-house, wherever we go, *is* ours, for it belongs to the community, and it is absolutely a home to us for the time being. It is usually the best house in the village, the prettiest and cosiest, where all the houses are so pretty and cosey. There is always another building for public meetings, called the temple, which is the

principal edifice, marble and classic and tasteful, which
we see almost as much of as the guest-house, for the
news of the Emissary's return has preceded him, and
everybody is alive with curiosity, and he has to stand
and deliver in the village temples everywhere. Of
course I am the great attraction, and after being scared
by it at first I have rather got to like it; the people are
so kind, and unaffected, and really delicate.

You mustn't get the notion that the Altrurians are a
solemn people at all; they are rather gay, and they like
other people's jokes as well as their own; I am sure
Mr. Makely, with his sense of humor, would be at home
with them at once. The one thing that more than any
other has helped them to conceive of the American
situation is its being the gigantic joke which we often
feel it to be; I don't know but it appears to them more
grotesque than it does to us even. At first, when Aristides would explain some peculiarity of ours, they
would receive him with a gale of laughing, but this
might change into cries of horror and pity later. One
of the things that amused and then revolted them
most was our patriotism. They thought it the drollest
thing in the world that men should be willing to give
their own lives and take the lives of other men for the
sake of a country which assured them no safety from
want, and did not even assure them work, and in
which they had no more logical interest than the
country they were going to fight. They could understand how a rich man might volunteer for one of our
wars, but when they were told that most of our volun-
teers were poor men, who left their mothers and sisters,
or their wives and children, without any means of support, except their meagre pay, they were quite bewildered and stopped laughing, as if the thing had passed
a joke. They asked, "How if one of these citizen

soldiers was killed?" and they seemed to suppose that in this case the country would provide for his family and give them work, or if the children were too young would support them at the public expense. It made me creep a little when my husband answered that the family of a crippled or invalided soldier would have a pension of eight or ten or fifteen dollars a month; and when they came back with the question why the citizens of such a country should love it enough to die for it, I could not have said why for the life of me. But Aristides, who is so magnificently generous, tried to give them a notion of the sublimity which is at the bottom of our illogicality and which adjusts so many apparently hopeless points of our anomaly. They asked how this sublimity differed from that of the savage who brings in his game and makes a feast for the whole tribe, and leaves his wife and children without provision against future want; but Aristides told them that there were essential differences between the Americans and savages, which arose from the fact that the savage condition was permanent and the American conditions were unconsciously provisional.

They are quite well informed about our life in some respects, but they wished to hear at first hand whether certain things were really so or not. For instance, they wanted to know whether people were allowed to marry and bring children into the world if they had no hopes of supporting them or educating them, or whether diseased people were allowed to become parents. In Altruria, you know, the families are generally small, only two or three children at the most, so that the parents can devote themselves to them the more fully; and as there is no fear of want here, the state interferes only when the parents are manifestly unfit to bring the little ones up. They imagined that there was something of that kind with us, but when they heard that the state interfered in the family only when the children were unruly, and then it punished the children by sending them to a reform school and disgracing them for life, instead of holding the parents accountable, they seemed to think that it was one of the most anomalous features of our great anomaly. Here, when the father and mother are always quarrelling, the children are taken from them, and the pair are separated, at first for a time, but after several chances for reform they are parted permanently.

But I must not give you the notion that all our conferences are so serious. Many have merely the character of social entertainments, which are not made here for invited guests, but for any who choose to come; all are welcome. At these there are often plays given by amateurs, and improvised from plots which supply the outline, while the performers supply the dialogue and action, as in the old Italian comedies. The Altrurians are so quick and fine, in fact, that they often remind me of the Italians more than any other people. One night there was for my benefit an American play, as the Altrurians imagined it from what they had read about us, and they had costumed it from the pictures of us they had seen in the newspapers Aristides had sent home while he was with us. The effect was a good deal like that American play which the Japanese company of Sada Yacco gave while it was in New York. It was all about a millionaire's daughter, who was loved by a poor young man and escaped with him to Altruria in an open boat from New York. The millionaire could be distinctly recognized by the dollar-marks which covered him all over, as they do in the caricatures of rich men in our yellow journals. It was funny to the last degree. In the last act he was seen giving his millions away to poor people, whose multitude was represented by the continually coming and going of four or five performers in and out of the door, in outrageously ragged clothes. The Altrurians have not yet imagined the nice degrees of poverty which we have achieved, and they could not have understood that a man with a hundred thousand dollars would have seemed poor to that multimillionaire. In fact, they do not grasp the idea of money at all. I heard afterwards that in the usual version the millionaire commits suicide in despair, but the piece had been given a happy ending out of kindness to me. I must say that in spite of the monstrous misconception the acting was extremely good, especially that of some comic characters.

But dancing is the great national amusement in Altruria, where it has not altogether lost its religious nature. A sort of march in the temples is as much a part of the worship as singing, and so dancing has been preserved from the disgrace which it used to be in with serious people among us. In the lovely afternoons you see young people dancing in the meadows, and hear them shouting in time to the music, while the older men and women watch them from their seats in the shade. Every sort of pleasure here is improvised, and as you pass through a village the first thing you know the young girls and young men start up in a sort of *girandole,* and linking hands in an endless chain stretch the figure along through the street and out over the highway to the next village, and the next and the next. The work has all been done in the forenoon, and every one who chooses is at liberty to join in the fun.

The villages are a good deal alike to a stranger, and we knew what to expect there after a while, but the country is perpetually varied, and the unexpected is always happening in it. The old railroad-beds, on which we travelled, are planted with fruit and nut trees and flowering shrubs, and our progress is through a fragrant bower that is practically endless, except where it takes the shape of a colonnade near the entrance of a village, with vines trained about white pillars, and clusters of grapes (which are ripening just now) hanging down. The change in the climate created by cutting off the southeastern peninsula and letting in the equatorial current, which was begun under the first Altrurian president, with an unexpended war-appropriation, and finished for what one of the old capitalistic wars used to cost, is something perfectly astonishing. Aristides says he told you something about it in his speech at the White Mountains, but you would never believe it without the evidence of your senses. Whole regions to the southward, which were nearest the pole and were sheeted with ice and snow, with the temperature and vegetation of Labrador, now have the climate of Italy; and the mountains, which used to bear nothing but glaciers, are covered with olive orchards and plantations of the delicious coffee which they drink here. Aristides says you could have the same results at home —no! *in the United States*—by cutting off the western shore of Alaska and letting in the Japanese current; and it could be done at the cost of any average war.

VI

But I must not get away from my personal experiences in these international statistics. Sometimes, when night overtakes us, we stop and camp beside the road, and set about getting our supper of eggs and bread and butter and cheese, or the fruits that are ripening all round us. Since my experience with that pullet I go meekly mushrooming in the fields and pastures; and when I have set the mushrooms stewing over an open fire, Aristides makes the coffee, and in a little while we have a banquet fit for kings—or for the poor things in every grade below them that serve kings, political or financial or industrial. There is always water, for it is brought down from the snow-fields of the mountains —there is not much rainfall—and carried in little concrete channels along the road-side from village to village, something like those conduits the Italian peasants use to bring down the water from the Maritime Alps to their fields and orchards; and you hear the soft gurgle of it the whole night long, and day long, too, whenever you stop. After supper we can read awhile by our electric lamp (we tap the current in the telephone wires anywhere), or Aristides sacrifices himself to me in a lesson of Altrurian grammar. Then we creep back into our van and fall asleep with the Southern Cross glittering over our heads. It is perfectly safe, though it was a long time before I could imagine the perfect safety of it. In a country where there are no thieves, because a thief here would not know what to do with his booty, we are secure from human molestation, and the land has long been cleared of all sorts of wild beasts, without being unpleasantly tamed. It is like England in that, and yet it has a touch of the sylvan, which you feel nowhere as you do in our dear New England hill country. There was one night, however, when we were lured on and on, and did not stop to camp till fairly in the dusk. Then we went to sleep without supper, for we had had rather a late lunch and were not hungry, and about one o'clock in the morning I was awakened by voices speaking Altrurian together. I recognized my husband's voice, which is always so kind, but which seemed to have a peculiarly tender and compassionate note in it now. The other was lower and of a sadness which wrung my heart, though I did not know in the least what the person was saying. The talk went on a long time, at first about some matter of immediate interest, as I fancied, and then apparently it branched off on some topic which seemed to concern the stranger, whoever he was. Then it seemed to get more indistinct, as if the stranger were leaving us and Aristides were going a little way with him. Presently I heard him coming back, and he put his head in at the van curtains, as if to see whether I was asleep.

"Well?" I said, and he said how sorry he was for having waked me. "Oh, I don't mind," I said. "Whom were you talking with? He had the saddest voice I ever heard. What did he want?"

"Oh, it seems that we are not far from the ruins of one of the old capitalistic cities, which have been left for a sort of warning against the former conditions, and he wished to caution us against the malarial influences from it. I think perhaps we had better push on a little way, if you don't mind."

165

The moon was shining clearly, and of course I did not mind, and Aristides got his hand on the lever, and we were soon getting out of the dangerous zone. " I think," he said, " they ought to abolish that pest-hole. I doubt if it serves any good purpose, now, though it has been useful in times past as an object-lesson."

" But who was your unknown friend ?" I asked, a great deal more curious about him than about the capitalistic ruin.

" Oh, just a poor murderer," he answered easily, and I shuddered back:

" A murderer !"

" Yes. He killed his friend some fifteen years ago in a jealous rage, and he is pursued by remorse that gives him no peace."

" And is the remorse his only punishment ?" I asked, rather indignantly.

" Isn't that enough ? God seemed to think it was, in the case of the first murderer, who killed his brother. All that he did to Cain was to set a mark on him. But we have not felt sure that we have the right to do this. We let God mark him, and He has done it with this man in the sorrow of his face. I was rather glad you couldn't see him, my dear. It is an awful face."

I confess that this sounded like mere sentimentalism to me, and I said, " Really, Aristides, I can't follow you. How are innocent people to be protected against this wretch, if he wanders about among them at will ?"

" They are as safe from him as from any other man in Altruria. His case was carefully looked into by the medical authorities, and it was decided that he was perfectly sane, so that he could be safely left at large, to expiate his misdeed in the only possible way that such a misdeed can be expiated—by doing good to others. What would you have had us do with him?"

The question rather staggered me, but I said, "He ought to have been imprisoned at least a year for manslaughter."

"Cain was not imprisoned an hour."

"That was a very different thing. But suppose you let a man go at large who has killed his friend in a jealous rage, what do you do with other murderers?"

"In Altruria there can be no other murderers. People cannot kill here for money, which prompts every other kind of murder in capitalistic countries, as well as every other kind of crime. I know, my dear, that this seems very strange to you, but you will accustom yourself to the idea, and then you will see the reasonableness of the Altrurian plan. On the whole, I am sorry you could not have seen that hapless man, and heard him. He had a face like death—"

"And a voice like death, too!" I put in.

"You noticed that? He wanted to talk about his crime with me. He wants to talk about it with any one who will listen to him. He is consumed with an undying pity for the man he slew. That is the first thing, the only thing, in his mind. If he could, I believe he would give his life for the life he took at any moment. But you cannot recreate one life by destroying another. There is no human means of ascertaining justice, but we can always do mercy with divine omniscience." As he spoke the sun pierced the edge of the eastern horizon, and lit up the marble walls and roofs of the Regionic capital which we were approaching.

At the meeting we had there in the afternoon, Aristides reported our having been warned against our

167

danger in the night by that murderer, and public record of the fact was made. The Altrurians consider any sort of punishment which is not expiation a far greater sin than the wrong it visits, and altogether barren and useless. After the record in this case had been made, the conference naturally turned upon what Aristides had seen of the treatment of criminals in America, and when he told of our prisons, where people merely arrested and not yet openly accused are kept, I did not know which way to look, for you know I am still an American at heart, Dolly. Did you ever see the inside of one of our police-stations at night? Or smell it? I did, once, when I went to give bail for a wretched girl who had been my servant, and had gone wrong, but had been arrested for theft, and I assure you that the sight and the smell woke me in the night for a month afterwards, and I have never quite ceased to dream about it.

The Altrurians listened in silence, and I hoped they could not realize the facts, though the story was every word true; but what seemed to make them the most indignant was the treatment of the families of the prisoners in what we call our penitentiaries and reformatories. At first they did not conceive of it, apparently, because it was so stupidly barbarous; they have no patience with stupidity; and when Aristides had carefully explained, it seemed as if they could not believe it. They thought it right that the convicts should be made to work, but they could not understand that the state really took away their wages, and left their families to suffer for want of the support which it had deprived them of. They said this was punishing the mothers and sisters, the wives and children of the prisoners, and was like putting out the eyes of an offender's innocent relatives as they had read was done

168

in Oriental countries. They asked if there was never any sort of protest against such an atrocious perversion of justice, and when the question was put to me I was obliged to own that I had never heard the system even criticised. Perhaps it has been, but I spoke only from my own knowledge.

VII

WELL, to get away from these dismal experiences, and come back to our travels, with their perpetual novelty, and the constantly varying beauty of the country!

The human interest of the landscape, that is always the great interest of it, and I wish I could make you feel it as I have felt it in this wonderful journey of ours. It is like the New England landscape at times, in its kind of gentle wildness, but where it has been taken back into the hand of man, how different the human interest is! Instead of a rheumatic old farmer, in his clumsy clothes, with some of his gaunt girls to help him, or perhaps his ageing wife, getting in the hay of one of those sweet meadows, and looking like so many animated scarecrows at their work; or instead of some young farmer, on the seat of his clattering mower, or mounted high over his tedder, but as much alone as if there were no one else in the neighborhood, silent and dull, or fierce or sullen, as the case might be, the work is always going on with companies of mowers or reapers, or planters, that chatter like birds or sing like them.

It is no use my explaining again and again that in a country like this, where everybody works, nobody *over* works, and that when the few hours of obligatory labor are passed in the mornings, people need not do anything unless they choose. Their working-dresses are very simple, but in all sorts of gay colors, like those you saw in the Greek play at Harvard, with straw hats for the men, and fillets of ribbon for the girls, and sandals for both. I speak of girls, for most of the married women are at home gardening, or about the household work, but men of every age work in the fields. The earth is dear to them because they get their life from it by labor that is not slavery; they come to love it every acre, every foot, because they have known it from childhood; and I have seen old men, very old, pottering about the orchards and meadows during the hours of voluntary work, and trimming them up here and there, simply because they could not keep away from the place, or keep their hands off the trees and bushes. Sometimes in the long, tender afternoons, we see far up on some pasture slope, groups of girls scattered about on the grass, with their sewing, or listening to some one reading. Other times they are giving a little play, usually a comedy, for life is so happy here that tragedy would not be true to it, with the characters coming and going in a grove of small pines, for the *coulisses,* and using a level of grass for the stage. If we stop, one of the audience comes down to us and invites us to come up and see the play, which keeps on in spite of the sensation that I can feel I make among them.

Everywhere the news of us has gone before us, and there is a universal curiosity to get a look at Aristides' capitalistic wife, as they call me. I made him translate it, and he explained that the word was merely descriptive and not characteristic; some people distinguished and called me American. There was one place where they were having a picnic in the woods up a hillside, and they asked us to join them, so we turned our van into the roadside and followed the procession. It was headed by two old men playing on pipes, and after

171

these came children singing, and then all sorts of people, young and old. When we got to an open place in the woods, where there was a spring, and smooth grass, they built fires, and began to get ready for the feast, while some of them did things to amuse the rest. Every one could do something; if you can imagine a party of artists, it was something like that. I should say the Altrurians had artists' manners, free, friendly, and easy, with a dash of humor in everything, and a wonderful willingness to laugh and make laugh. Aristides is always explaining that the artist is their ideal type; that is, some one who works gladly, and plays as gladly as he works; no one here is asked to do work that he hates, unless he seems to hate every kind of work. When this happens, the authorities find out something for him that he had *better* like, by letting him starve till he works. That picnic lasted the whole afternoon and well into the night, and then the picnickers went home through the starlight, leading the little ones, or carrying them when they were too little or too tired. But first they came down to our van with us, and sang us a serenade after we had disappeared into it, and then left us, and sent their voices back to us out of the dark.

One morning at dawn, as we came into a village, we saw nearly the whole population mounting the marble steps of the temple, all the holiday dress of the Voluntaries, which they put on here every afternoon when the work is done. Last of the throng came a procession of children, looking something like a May-Day party, and midway of their line were a young man and a young girl, hand in hand, who parted at the door of the temple, and entered separately. Aristides called out, " Oh, it is a wedding! You are in luck, Eveleth," and then and there I saw my first Altrurian wedding.

172

Within, the pillars and the altar and the seats of the elders were garlanded with flowers, so fresh and fragrant that they seemed to have blossomed from the marble overnight, and there was a soft murmur of Altrurian voices that might very well have seemed the hum of bees among the blossoms. This subsided, as the young couple, who had paused just inside the temple door, came up the middle side by side, and again separated and took their places, the youth on the extreme right of the elder, and the maiden on the extreme left of the eldresses, and stood facing the congregation, which was also on foot, and joined in the hymn which everybody sang. Then one of the eldresses rose and began a sort of statement which Aristides translated to me afterwards. She said that the young couple whom we saw there had for the third time asked to become man and wife, after having believed for a year that they loved each other, and having statedly come before the marriage authorities and been questioned as to the continuance of their affection. She said that probably every one present knew that they had been friends from childhood, and none would be surprised that they now wished to be united for life. They had been carefully instructed as to the serious nature of the marriage bond, and admonished as to the duties they were entering into, not only to each other, but to the community. At each successive visit to the authorities they had been warned, separately and together, against the danger of trusting to anything like a romantic impulse, and they had faithfully endeavored to act upon this advice, as they testified. In order to prove the reality of their affection, they had been parted every third month, and had lived during that time in different Regions where it was meant they should meet many other young people, so that if they

173

felt any swerving of the heart they might not persist in an intention which could only bring them final unhappiness. It seems this is the rule in the case of young lovers, and people usually marry very young here, but if they wish to marry later in life the rule is not enforced so stringently, or not at all. The bride and groom we saw had both stood these trials, and at each return they had been more and more sure that they loved each other, and loved no one else. Now they were here to unite their hands, and to declare the union of their hearts before the people.

Then the eldress sat down and an elder arose, who bade the young people come forward to the centre of the line, where the elders and eldresses were sitting. He took his place behind them, and once more and for the last time he conjured them not to persist if they felt any doubt of themselves. He warned them that if they entered into the married state, and afterwards repented to the point of seeking divorce, the divorce would indeed be granted them, but on terms, as they must realize, of lasting grief to themselves through the offence they would commit against the commonwealth. They answered that they were sure of themselves, and ready to exchange their troth for life and death. Then they joined hands, and declared that they took each other for husband and wife. The congregation broke into another hymn and slowly dispersed, leaving the bride and groom with their families, who came up to them and embraced them, pressing their cheeks against the cheeks of the young pair.

This ended the solemnity, and then the festivity began, as it ended, with a wedding feast, where people sang and danced and made speeches and drank toasts, and the fun was kept up till the hours of the Obligatories approached; and then, what do you think? The

174

married pair put off their wedding garments with the
rest and went to work in the fields! Later, I understood, if they wished to take a wedding journey they
could freely do so; but the first thing in their married
life they must honor the Altrurian ideal of work, by
which every one must live in order that every other
may live without overwork. I believe that the marriage ceremonial is something like that of the Quakers,
but I never saw a Quaker wedding, and I could only
compare this with the crazy romps with which our
house-weddings often end, with throwing of rice and
old shoes, and tying ribbons to the bridal carriage and
baggage, and following the pair to the train with out-
breaks of tiresome hilarity, which make them conspicu-
ous before their fellow - travellers; or with some of
our ghastly church weddings, in which the religious
ceremonial is lost in the social effect, and ends with that
everlasting thumping march from "Lohengrin," and
the outsiders storming about the bridal pair and the
guests with the rude curiosity that the fattest policemen at the canopied and carpeted entrance cannot
check.

12

VIII

W̞ᴇ have since been at other weddings and at christenings and at funerals. The ceremonies are always held in the temples, and are always in the same serious spirit. As the Altrurians are steadfast believers in immortality, there is a kind of solemn elevation in the funeral ceremonies which I cannot give you a real notion of. It is helped, I think, by the custom of not performing the ceremony over the dead; a brief rite is reserved for the cemetery, where it is wished that the kindred shall not be present, lest they think always of the material body and not of the spiritual body which shall be raised in incorruption. Religious service is held in the temples every day at the end of the Obligatories, and whenever we are near a village or in any of the capitals we always go. It is very simple. After a hymn, to which the people sometimes march round the interior of the temple, each lays on the altar an offering from the fields or woods where they have been working, if it is nothing but a head of grain or a wild flower or a leaf. Then any one is at liberty to speak, but any one else may go out without offence. There is no ritual; sometimes they read a chapter from the New Testament, preferably a part of the story of Christ or a passage from His discourses. The idea of coming to the temple at the end of the day's labor is to consecrate that day's work, and they do not call anything work that is not work with the hands. When I explained, or tried to explain, that among us a great many people worked

176

with their brains, to amuse others or to get handwork out of them, they were unable to follow me. I asked if they did not consider composing music or poetry or plays, or painting pictures work, and they said, No, that was pleasure, and must be indulged only during the Voluntaries; it was never to be honored like work with the hands, for it would not equalize the burden of that, but might put an undue share of it on others. They said that lives devoted to such pursuits must be very unwholesome, and they brought me to book about the lives of most artists, literary men, and financiers in the capitalistic world to prove what they said. They held that people must work with their hands willingly, in the artistic spirit, but they could only do that when they knew that others differently gifted were working in like manner with their hands.

I couldn't begin to tell you all our queer experiences. As I have kept saying, I am a great curiosity everywhere, and I could flatter myself that people were more eager to see me than to hear Aristides. Sometimes I couldn't help thinking that they expected to find me an awful warning, a dreadful example of whatever a woman ought not to be, and a woman from capitalistic conditions *must* be logically. But sometimes they were very intelligent, even the simplest villagers, as we should call them, though there is such an equality of education and opportunity here that no simplicity of life has the effect of dulling people as it has with us. One thing was quite American: they always wanted to know how I liked Altruria, and when I told them, as I sincerely could, that I adored it, they were quite affecting in their pleasure. They generally asked if I would like to go back to America, and when I said No, they were delighted beyond anything. They said I must become a citizen and vote and take part in the government, for

177

that was every woman's duty as well as right; it was wrong to leave the whole responsibility to the men. They asked if American women took no interest in the government, and when I told them there was a very small number who wished to influence politics socially, as the Englishwomen did, but without voting or taking any responsibility, they were shocked. In one of the Regionic capitals they wanted me to speak after Aristides, but I had nothing prepared; at the next I did get off a little speech in English, which he translated after me. Later he put it into Altrurian, and I memorized it, and made myself immensely popular by parroting it.

The pronunciation of Altrurian is not difficult, for it is spelled phonetically, and the sounds are very simple. Where they were once difficult they have been simplified, for here the simplification of life extends to everything; and the grammar has been reduced in its structure till it is as elemental as English grammar or Norwegian. The language is Greek in origin, but the intricate inflections and the declensions have been thrown away, and it has kept only the simplest forms. You must get Mr. Twelvemough to explain this to you, Dolly, for it would take me too long, and I have so much else to tell you. A good many of the women have taken up English, but they learn it as a dead language, and they give it a comical effect by trying to pronounce it as it is spelled.

I suppose you are anxious, if these letters which are piling up and piling up should ever reach you, or even start to do so, to know something about the Altrurian cities, and what they are like. Well, in the first place, you must cast all images of American cities out of your mind, or any European cities, except, perhaps, the prettiest and stateliest parts of Paris, where there is a regular sky-line, and the public buildings and monuments are approached through shaded avenues. There are no private houses here, in our sense — that is, houses which people have built with their own money on their own land, and made as ugly outside and as molestive to their neighbors and the passers-by as they chose. As the buildings belong to the whole people, the first requirement is that they shall be beautiful inside and out. There are a few grand edifices looking like Greek temples, which are used for the government offices, and these are, of course, the most dignified, but the dwellings are quite as attractive and comfortable. They are built round courts, with gardens and flowers in the courts, and wide grassy spaces round them. They are rather tall, but never so tall as our great hotels or apartment-houses, and the floors are brought to one level by elevators, which are used only in the capitals; and, generally speaking, I should say the villages were pleasanter than the cities. In fact, the village is the Altrurian ideal, and there is an effort everywhere to reduce the size of the towns and increase the number of the villages. The outlying farms have been gathered into those, and now there is not one of those lonely places in the country, like those where our farmers toil alone outdoors and their wives alone indoors, and both go mad so often in the solitude. The villages are almost in sight of each other, and the people go to their fields in company, while the women carry on their housekeeping co-operatively, with a large kitchen which they use in common; they have their meals apart or together, as they like. If any one is sick or disabled the neighbors come in and help do her work, as they used with us in the early times, and as they still do in country places. Village life here is preferred, just as country life is in England, and one thing that will amuse you, with your American ideas, and your pride in the overgrowth of our cities: the Altrurian papers solemnly announce from time to time that the population of such or such a capital has been reduced so many hundreds or thousands since the last census. That means that the villages in the neighborhood have been increased in number and population.

Meanwhile, I must say the capitals are delightful: clean, airy, quiet, with the most beautiful architecture, mostly classic and mostly marble, with rivers running through them and round them, and every real convenience, but not a clutter of artificial conveniences, as with us. In the streets there are noiseless trolleys (where they have not been replaced by public automobiles) which the long distances of the ample groundplan make rather necessary, and the rivers are shot over with swift motor-boats; for the short distances you always expect to walk, or if you don't expect it, you walk anyway. The car-lines and boat-lines are public, and they are free, for the Altrurians think that the community owes transportation to every one who lives beyond easy reach of the points which their work calls them to.

Of course the great government stores are in the capitals, and practically there are no stores in the villages, except for what you might call emergency supplies. But you must not imagine, Dolly, that shopping, here, is like shopping at home—or in America, as I am learning to say, for Altruria is home now. That is, you don't fill your purse with bank-notes, or have things charged. You get everything you want, within reason, and certainly everything you need, for nothing. You have only to provide yourself with a card, something like that you have to show at the Army and Navy Stores in London, when you first go to buy there, which certifies that you belong to this or that working-phalanx, and that you have not failed in the Obligatories for such and such a length of time. If you are not entitled to this card, you had better not go shopping, for there is no possible equivalent for it which will enable you to carry anything away or have it sent to your house. At first I could not help feeling rather indignant when I was asked to show my work-card in the stores; I had usually forgotten to bring it, or sometimes I had brought my husband's card, which would not do at all, unless I could say that I had been ill or disabled, for a woman is expected to work quite the same as a man. Of course her housework counts, and as we are on a sort of public mission, they count our hours of travel as working-hours, especially as Aristides has made it a point of good citizenship for us to stop every now and then and join in the Obligatories when the villagers were getting in the farm crops or quarrying stone or putting up a house. I am never much use in quarrying or building, but I come in strong in the hay-fields or the apple orchards or the orange groves.

The shopping here is not so enslaving as it is with us—I mean, with *you*—because the fashions do not change, and you get things only when you need them, not when you want them, or when other people think you do. The costume was fixed long ago, when the Altrurian era began, by a commission of artists, and it would be considered very bad form as well as bad morals to try changing it in the least. People are allowed to choose their own colors, but if one goes very wrong, or so far wrong as to offend the public taste, she is gently admonished by the local art commission; if she insists, they let her have her own way, but she seldom wants it when she knows that people think her a fright. Of course the costume is modified somewhat

181

for the age and shape of the wearer, but this is not so often as you might think. There are no very lean or very stout people, though there are old and young, just as there are with us. But the Altrurians keep young very much longer than capitalistic peoples do, and the life of work keeps down their weight. You know I used to incline a little to over-plumpness, I really believe because I overate at times simply to keep from thinking of the poor who had to undereat, but that is quite past now; I have lost at least twenty-five pounds from working out-doors and travelling so much and living very, very simply.

IX

I HAVE to jot things down as they come into my mind, and I am afraid I forget some of the most important. Everybody is so novel on this famous tour of ours that I am continually interested, but one has one's preferences even in Altruria, and I believe I like best the wives of the artists and literary men whom one finds working in the galleries and libraries of the capitals everywhere. They are not more intelligent than other women, perhaps, but they are more sympathetic; and one sees so little of those people in New York, for all they abound there.

The galleries are not only for the exhibition of pictures, but each has numbers of ateliers, where the artists work and teach. The libraries are the most wonderfully imagined things. You do not have to come and study in them, but if you are working up any particular subject, the books relating to it are sent to your dwelling every morning and brought away every noon, so that during the obligatory hours you have them completely at your disposition, and during the Voluntaries you can consult them with the rest of the public in the library; it is not thought best that study should be carried on throughout the day, and the results seem to justify this theory. If you want to read a book merely for pleasure, you are allowed to take it out and live with it as long as you like; the copy you have is immediately replaced with another, so that you

183

do not feel hurried and are not obliged to ramp through it in a week or a fortnight.

The Altrurian books are still rather sealed books to me, but they are delightful to the eye, all in large print on wide margins, with flexible bindings, and such light paper that you can hold them in one hand indefinitely without tiring. I must send you some with this, if I ever get my bundle of letters off to you. You will see by the dates that I am writing you one every day; I had thought of keeping a journal for you, but then I should have had left out a good many things that happened during our first days, when the impressions were so vivid, and I should have got to addressing my records to myself, and I think I had better keep to the form of letters. If they reach you, and you read them at random, why that is very much the way I write them.

I despair of giving you any *real* notion of the capitals, but if you remember the White City at the Columbian Fair at Chicago in 1893, you can have some idea of the general effect of one; only there is nothing heterogeneous in their beauty. There is one classic rule in the architecture, but each of the different architects may characterize an edifice from himself, just as different authors writing the same language characterize it by the diction natural to him. There are suggestions of the capitals in some of our cities, and if you remember Commonwealth Avenue in Boston, you can imagine something like the union of street and garden which every street of them is. The trolleys run under the overarching trees between the lawns, flanked by gravelled footpaths between flower-beds, and you take the cars or not as you like. As there is no hurry, they go about as fast as English trams, and the danger from them is practically reduced to nothing by the crossings

184

dipping under them at the street corners. The centre of the capital is approached by colonnades, which at night bear groups of great bulbous lamps, and by day flutter with the Altrurian and Regionic flags. Around this centre are the stores and restaurants and theatres, and galleries and libraries, with arcades over the sidewalks, like those in Bologna; sometimes the arcades are in two stories, as they are in Chester. People are constantly coming and going in an easy way during the afternoon, though in the morning the streets are rather deserted.

But what is the use? I could go on describing and describing, and never get in half the differences from American cities, with their hideous uproar, and their mud in the wet, and their clouds of swirling dust in the wind. But there is one feature which I must mention, because you can fancy it from the fond dream of a great national highway which some of our architects projected while they were still in the fervor of excitement from the beauty of the Peristyle, and other features of the White City. They really have such a highway here, crossing the whole Altrurian continent, and uniting the circle of the Regionic capitals. As we travelled for a long time by the country roads on the beds of the old railways, I had no idea of this magnificent avenue, till one day my husband suddenly ran our van into the one leading up to the first capital we were to visit. Then I found myself between miles and miles of stately white pillars, rising and sinking as the road found its natural levels, and growing in the perspective before us and dwindling behind us. I could not keep out of my mind a colonnade of palm-trees, only the fronds were lacking, and there were never palms so beautiful. Each pillar was inscribed with the name of some Altrurian who had done something for his country, written some beautiful poem or story, or history, made some scientific discovery, composed an opera, invented a universal convenience, performed a wonderful cure, or been a delightful singer, or orator, or gardener, or farmer. Not one soldier, general or admiral, among them! That seemed very strange to me, and I asked Aristides how it was. Like everything else in Altruria, it was very simple; there had been no war for so long that there were no famous soldiers to commemorate. But he stopped our van when he came to the first of the many arches which spanned the highway, and read out to me in English the Altrurian record that it was erected in honor of the first President of the Altrurian Commonwealth, who managed the negotiations when the capitalistic oligarchies to the north and south were peacefully annexed, and the descendants of the three nations joined in the commemoration of an event that abolished war forever on the Altrurian continent.

Here I can imagine Mr. Makely asking who footed the bills for this beauty and magnificence, and whether these works were constructed at the cost of the nation, or the different Regions, or the abuttors on the different highways. But the fact is, you poor, capitalistic dears, they cost nobody a dollar, for there is not a dollar in Altruria. You must worry into the idea somehow that in Altruria you cannot buy anything except by *working,* and that work is the current coin of the republic: you pay for everything by drops of sweat, and off your own brow, not somebody else's brow. The people built these monuments and colonnades, and aqueducts and highways and byways, and sweet villages and palatial cities with their own hands, after the designs of artists, who also took part in the labor. But it was a labor that they delighted in so much that they chose to perform

186

it during the Voluntaries, when they might have been resting, and not during the Obligatories, when they were required to work. So it was all joy and all glory. They say there never was such happiness in any country since the world began. While the work went on it was like a perpetual Fourth of July or an everlasting picnic.

But I know you hate this sort of economical stuff, Dolly, and I will make haste to get down to business, as Mr. Makely would say, for I am really coming to something that you will think worth while. One morning, when we had made half the circle of the capitals, and were on the homestretch to the one where we had left our dear mother—for Aristides claims her, too— and I was letting that dull nether anxiety for her come to the top, though we had had the fullest telephonic talks with her every day, and knew she was well and happy, we came round the shoulder of a wooded cliff and found ourselves on an open stretch of the northern coast. At first I could only exclaim at the beauty of the sea, lying blue and still beyond a long beach closed by another headland, and I did not realize that a large yacht which I saw close to land had gone ashore. The beach was crowded with Altrurians, who seemed to have come to the rescue, for they were putting off to the yacht in boats and returning with passengers, and jumping out, and pulling their boats with them up on to the sand.

I was quite bewildered, and I don't know what to say I was the next thing, when I saw that the stranded yacht was flying the American flag from her peak. I supposed she must be one of our cruisers, she was so large, and the first thing that flashed into my mind was a kind of amused wonder what those poor Altrurians would do with a ship-of-war and her marines and crew. I couldn't ask any coherent questions, and luckily Aristides was answering my incoherent ones in the best possible way by wheeling our van down on the beach and making for the point nearest the yacht. He had time to say he did not believe she was a government vessel, and, in fact, I remembered that once I had seen a boat in the North River getting up steam to go to Europe which was much larger, and had her decks covered with sailors that I took for bluejackets; but she was only the private yacht of some people I knew.

These stupid things kept going and coming in my mind while my husband was talking with some of the Altrurian girls who were there helping with the men. They said that the yacht had gone ashore the night before last in one of the sudden fogs that come up on that coast, and that some people whom the sailors seemed to obey were camping on the edge of the upland above the beach, under a large tent they had brought from the yacht. They had refused to go to the guest-house in the nearest village, and as nearly as the girls could make out they expected the yacht to get afloat from tide to tide, and then intended to re-embark on her. In the mean time they had provisioned themselves from the ship, and were living in a strange way of their own. Some of them seemed to serve the others, but these appeared to be used with a very ungrateful indifference, as if they were of a different race. There was one who wore a white apron and white cap who directed the cooking for the rest, and had several assistants; and from time to time very disagreeable odors came from the camp, like burning flesh. The Altrurians had carried them fruits and vegetables, but the men-assistants had refused them contemptuously and seemed suspicious of the variety of mushrooms they offered them. They called out, " To-stoo!" and I understood that the strangers were afraid they were bringing toadstools. One of the Altrurian girls had been studying English in the nearest capital, and she had tried to talk with these people, pronouncing it in the Altrurian way, but they could make nothing of one another; then she wrote down what she wanted to say, but as she spelled it phonetically they were not able to read her English. She asked us if I was the American Altrurian she had heard of, and when I said yes she lost no time in showing us to the camp of the castaways.

As soon as we saw their tents we went forward till we were met at the largest by a sort of marine footman, who bowed slightly and said to me, "What name shall I say, ma'am?" and I answered distinctly, so that he might get the name right, "Mr. and Mrs. Homos." Then he held back the flap of the marquee, which seemed to serve these people as a drawing-room, and called out, standing very rigidly upright, to let us pass, in the way that I remembered so well, "Mr. and Mrs. 'Omos!" and a severe-looking, rather elderly lady rose to meet us with an air that was both anxious and forbidding, and before she said anything else she burst out, "You don't mean to say you speak English?"

I said that I spoke English, and had not spoken anything else but rather poor French until six months before, and then she demanded, "Have you been cast away on this outlandish place, too?"

I laughed and said I lived here, and I introduced my husband as well as I could without knowing her name. He explained with his pretty Altrurian accent, which you used to like so much, that we had ventured to come in the hope of being of use to them, and added some regrets for their misfortune so sweetly that I wondered she could help responding in kind. But she merely said, "Oh!" and then she seemed to recollect herself, and frowning to a very gentle-looking old man to come forward, she ignored my husband in presenting me. " Mr. Thrall, Mrs. ——"

She hesitated for my name, and I supplied it, " Homos," and as the old man had put out his hand in a kindly way I took it.

" And this is my husband, Aristides Homos, an Altrurian," I said, and then, as the lady had not asked us to sit down, or shown the least sign of liking our being there, the natural woman flamed up in me as she hadn't in all the time I have been away from New York. " I am glad you are so comfortable here, Mr. Thrall. You won't need us, I see. The people about will do anything in their power for you. Come, my dear," and I was sweeping out of that tent in a manner calculated to give the eminent millionaire's wife a notion of Altrurian hauteur which I must own would have been altogether mistaken.

I knew who they were perfectly. Even if I had not once met them I should have known that they were the ultra-rich Thralls, from the multitudinous pictures of them that I had seen in the papers at home, not long after they came on to New York.

He was beginning, " Oh no, oh no," but I cut in. " My husband and I are on our way to the next Regionic capital, and we are somewhat hurried. You will be quite well looked after by the neighbors here, and I see that we are rather in your housekeeper's way."

It *was* nasty, Dolly, and I won't deny it; it was *vulgar*. But what would *you* have done ? I could feel Aristides' mild eye sadly on me, and I was sorry for him, but I assure him I was not sorry for them, till that old man spoke again, so timidly: " It isn't my— it's my wife, Mrs. Homos. Let me introduce her. But haven't we met before ?"

"Perhaps during my first husband's lifetime. I was Mrs. Bellington Strange."

"Mrs. P. Bellington Strange? Your husband was a dear friend of mine when we were both young—a good man, if ever there was one; the best in the world! I am so glad to see you again. Ah—my dear, you remember my speaking of Mrs. Strange?"

He took my hand again and held it in his soft old hands, as if hesitating whether to transfer it to her, and my heart melted towards him. You may think it very odd, Dolly, but it was what he said of my dear, dead husband that softened me. It made him seem very fatherly, and I felt the affection for him that I felt for my husband, when he seemed more like a father. Aristides and I often talk of it, and he has no wish that I should forget him.

Mrs. Thrall made no motion to take my hand from him, but she said, "I think I have met Mr. Strange," and now I saw in the background, sitting on a camp-stool near a long, lank young man stretched in a hammock, a very handsome girl, who hastily ran through a book, and then dropped it at the third mention of my name. I suspected that the book was the Social Register, and that the girl's search for me had been satisfactory, for she rose and came vaguely towards us, while the young man unfolded himself from the hammock, and stood hesitating, but looking as if he rather liked what had happened.

Mr. Thrall bustled about for camp-stools, and said, "Do stop and have some breakfast with us, it's just coming in. May I introduce my daughter, Lady Moors and—and Lord Moors?" The girl took my hand, and the young man bowed from his place; but if that poor old man had known, peace was not to be made so easily between two such bad-tempered women as Mrs. Thrall and myself. We expressed some very stiff sentiments in regard to the weather, and the prospect of the yacht getting off with the next tide, and my husband joined in with that manly gentleness of his, but we did not sit down, much less offer to stay to breakfast. We had got to the door of the tent, the family following us, even to the noble son-in-law, and as she now realized that we are actually going, Mrs. Thrall gasped out, "But you are not *leaving* us? What shall we *do* with all these natives?"

This was again too much, and I flamed out at her. "*Natives!* They are cultivated and refined people, for they are Altrurians, and I assure you you will be in much better hands than mine with them, for I am only Altrurian by marriage!"

She was one of those leathery egotists that nothing will make a dint in, and she came back with, "But we don't speak the language, and they don't speak English, and how are we to manage if the yacht doesn't get afloat?"

"Oh, no doubt you will be looked after from the capital we have just left. But I will venture to make a little suggestion with regard to the natives in the mean time. They are not proud, but they are very sensitive, and if you fail in any point of consideration, they will understand that you do not want their hospitality."

"I imagine our own people will be able to look after us," she answered quite as nastily. "We do not propose to be dependent on them. We can pay our way here as we do elsewhere."

"The experiment will be worth trying," I said. "Come, Aristides!" and I took the poor fellow away with me to our van. Mr. Thrall made some hopeless little movements towards us, but I would not stop

or even look back. When we got into the van, I made
Aristides put on the full power, and fell back into my
seat and cried a while, and then I scolded him because
he would not scold me, and went on in a really scan-
dalous way. It must have been a revelation to him,
but he only smoothed me on the shoulder and said,
"Poor Eveleth, poor Eveleth," till I thought I should
scream; but it ended in my falling on his neck, and
saying I knew I was horrid, and what did he want me
to do?

After I calmed down into something like rationality,
he said he thought we had perhaps done the best thing
we could for those people in leaving them to themselves, for they could come to no possible harm among
the neighbors. He did not believe from what he had
seen of the yacht from the shore, and from what the
Altrurians had told him, that there was one chance
in a thousand of her ever getting afloat. But those
people would have to convince themselves of the fact,
and of several other facts in their situation. I asked him
what he meant, and he said he could tell me, but that
as yet it was a public affair, and he would rather not
anticipate the private interest I would feel in it. I did
not insist; in fact, I wanted to get that odious woman
out of my mind as soon as I could, for the thought of
her threatened to poison the pleasure of the rest of our
tour.

I believe my husband hurried it a little, though he
did not shorten it, and we got back to the Maritime
Region almost a week sooner than we had first intended. I found my dear mother well, and still serenely
happy in her Altrurian surroundings. She had begun to learn the language, and she had a larger acquaintance in the capital, I believe, than any other one
person. She said everybody had called on her, and

they were the kindest people she had ever dreamed of. She had exchanged cooking-lessons with one lady who, they told her, was a distinguished scientist, and she had taught another, who was a great painter, a peculiar embroidery stitch which she had learned from my grandmother, and which everybody admired. These two ladies had given her most of her grammatical instruction in Altrurian, but there was a bright little girl who had enlarged her vocabulary more than either, in helping her about her housework, the mother having lent her for the purpose. My mother said she was not ashamed to make blunders before a child, and the little witch had taken the greatest delight in telling her the names of things in the house and the streets and the fields outside the town, where they went long walks together.

X

WELL, my dear Dorothea, I had been hoping to go more into detail about my mother and about our life in the Maritime Capital, which is to be our home for a year, but I had hardly got down the last words when Aristides came in with a despatch from the Seventh Regionic, summoning us there on important public business: I haven't got over the feeling yet of being especially distinguished and flattered at sharing in public business; but the Altrurian women are so used to it that they do not think anything of it. The despatch was signed by an old friend of my husband's, Cyril Chrysostom, who had once been Emissary in England, and to whom my husband wrote his letters when he was in America. I hated to leave my mother so soon, but it could not be helped, and we took the first electric express for the Seventh Regionic, where we arrived in about an hour and forty minutes, making the three hundred miles in that time easily. I couldn't help regretting our comfortable van, but there was evidently haste in the summons, and I confess that I was curious to know what the matter was, though I had made a shrewd guess the first instant, and it turned out that I was not mistaken.

The long and the short of it was that there was trouble with the people who had come ashore in that yacht, and were destined never to go to sea in her. She was hopelessly bedded in the sand, and the waves that were breaking over her were burying her deeper and deeper. The owners were living in their tent as we had left them, and her crew were camped in smaller tents and any shelter they could get, along the beach. They had brought her stores away, but many of the provisions had been damaged, and it had become a pressing question what should be done about the people. We had been asked to consult with Cyril and his wife, and the other Regionic chiefs and their wives, and we threshed the question out nearly the whole night.

I am afraid it will appear rather comical in some aspects to you and Mr. Makely, but I can assure you that it was a very serious matter with the Altrurian authorities. If there had been any hope of a vessel from the capitalistic world touching at Altruria within a definite time, they could have managed, for they would have gladly kept the yacht's people and owners till they could embark them for Australia or New Zealand, and would have made as little of the trouble they were giving as they could. But until the trader that brought us should return with the crew, as the captain had promised, there was no ship expected, and any other wreck in the mean time would only add to their difficulty. You may be surprised, though I was not, that the difficulty was mostly with the yacht-owners, and above all with Mrs. Thrall, who had baffled every effort of the authorities to reduce what they considered the disorder of their life.

With the crew it was a different matter. As soon as they had got drunk on the wines and spirts they had brought from the wreck, and then had got sober because they had drunk all the liquors up, they began to be more manageable; when their provisions ran short, and they were made to understand that they would not be allowed to plunder the fields and woods, or loot the villages for something to eat, they became almost exemplarily do-

196

cile. At first they were disposed to show fight, and the principles of the Altrurians did not allow them to use violence in bringing them to subjection; but the men had counted without their hosts in supposing that they could therefore do as they pleased, unless they pleased to do right. After they had made their first foray they were warned by Cyril, who came from the capital to speak English with them, that another raid would not be suffered. They therefore attempted it by night, but the Altrurians were prepared for them with the flexible steel nets which are their only means of defence, and half a dozen sailors were taken in one. When they attempted to break out, and their shipmates attempted to break in to free them, a light current of electricity was sent through the wires and the thing was done. Those who were rescued — the Altrurians will not say captured—had hoes put into their hands the next morning, and were led into the fields and set to work, after a generous breakfast of coffee, bread, and mushrooms. The chickens they had killed in their midnight expedition were buried, and those which they had not killed lost no time in beginning to lay eggs for the sustenance of the reformed castaways. As an extra precaution with the " rescued," when they were put to work, each of them with a kind of shirt of mail, worn over his coat, which could easily be electrized by a metallic filament connecting with the communal dynamo, and under these conditions they each did a full day's work during the Obligatories.

As the short commons grew shorter and shorter, both meat and drink, at Camp Famine, and the campers found it was useless to attempt thieving from the Altrurians, they had tried begging from the owners in their large tent, but they were told that the provisions were giving out there, too, and there was nothing for them. When they insisted the servants of the owners had threatened them with revolvers, and the sailors, who had nothing but their knives, preferred to attempt living on the country. Within a week the whole crew had been put to work in the woods and fields and quarries, or wherever they could make themselves useful. They were, on the whole, so well fed and sheltered that they were perfectly satisfied, and went down with the Altrurians on the beach during the Voluntaries and helped secure the yacht's boats and pieces of wreckage that came ashore. Until they became accustomed or resigned to the Altrurian diet, they were allowed to catch shell - fish and the crabs that swarmed along the sand and cook them, but on condition that they built their fires on the beach, and cooked only during an offshore wind, so that the fumes of the roasting should not offend the villagers.

Cyril acknowledged, therefore, that the question of the crew was for the present practically settled, but Mr. and Mrs. Thrall, and their daughter and son-in-law, with their servants, still presented a formidable problem. As yet, their provisions had not run out, and they were living in their marquee as we had seen them three weeks earlier, just after their yacht went ashore. It could not be said that they were molestive in the same sense as the sailors, but they were even more demoralizing in the spectacle they offered the neighborhood of people dependent on hired service, and in their endeavors to supply themselves in perishable provisions, like milk and eggs, by means of money. Cyril had held several interviews with them, in which he had at first delicately intimated, and then explicitly declared, that the situation could not be prolonged. The two men had been able to get the Altrurian point of view in some measure, and so had Lady Moors, but Mrs. Thrall had remained stiffly obtuse and obstinate, and it was in despair of bringing her to terms without resorting to rescue that he had summoned us to help him.

It was not a pleasant job, but of course we could not refuse, and we agreed that as soon as we had caught a nap, and had a bite of breakfast we would go over to their camp with Cyril and his wife, and see what we could do with the obnoxious woman. I confess that I had some little consolation in the hope that I should see her properly humbled.

XI

Mr. Thrall and Lord Moors must have seen us
coming, for they met us at the door of the tent without the intervention of the footman, and gave us quite
as much welcome as we could expect in our mission, so disagreeable all round. Mr. Thrall was as
fatherly with me as before, and Lord Moors was as
polite to Cyril and Mrs. Chrysostom as could have
been wished. In fact he and Cyril were a sort of acquaintances from the time of Cyril's visit to England
where he met the late Earl Moors, the father of the
present peer, in some of his visits to Toynbee Hall, and
the Whitechapel Settlements. The earl was very much
interested in the slums, perhaps because he was rather
poor himself, if not quite slummy. The son was then
at the university, and when he came out and into his
title he so far shared his father's tastes that he came to
America; it was not slumming, exactly, but a nobleman
no doubt feels it to be something like it. After a
little while in New York he went out to Colorado,
where so many needy noblemen bring up, and there he
met the Thralls, and fell in love with the girl. Cyril
had understood—or rather Mrs. Cyril,—that it was
a love-match on both sides, but on Mrs. Thrall's
side it was business. He did not even speak of settlements—the English are *so* romantic when they *are*
romantic! — but Mr. Thrall saw to all that, and the
young people were married after a very short court-
ship. They spent their honeymoon partly in Colorado

Springs and partly in San Francisco, where the Thralls' yacht was lying, and then they set out on a voyage round the world, making stops at the interesting places, and bringing up on the beach of the Seventh Region of Altruria, en route for the eastern coast of South America. From that time on, Cyril said, we knew their history.

After Mr. Thrall had shaken hands tenderly with me, and cordially with Aristides, he said, " Won't you all come inside and have breakfast with us? My wife and daughter "—

" Thank you, Mr. Thrall," Cyril answered for us, " we will sit down here, if you please; and as your ladies are not used to business, we will not ask you to disturb them."

" I'm sure Lady Moors," the young nobleman began, but Cyril waved him silent.

" We shall be glad later, but not now! Gentlemen, I have asked my friends Aristides Homos and Eveleth Homos to accompany my wife and me this morning because Eveleth is an American, and will understand your position, and he has lately been in America and will be able to clarify the situation from both sides. We wish you to believe that we are approaching you in the friendliest spirit, and that nothing could be more painful to us than to seem inhospitable."

" Then why," the old man asked, with business-like promptness, " do you object to our presence here? I don't believe I get your idea."

" Because the spectacle which your life offers is contrary to good morals, and as faithful citizens we cannot countenance it."

" But in what way is our life immoral? I have always thought that I was a good citizen at home; at

201

least I can't remember having been arrested for disorderly conduct."

He smiled at me, as if I should appreciate the joke, and it hurt me to keep grave, but suspecting what a bad time he was going to have, I thought I had better not join him in any levity.

"I quite conceive you," Cyril replied. "But you present to our people, who are offended by it, the spectacle of dependence upon hireling service for your daily comfort and convenience."

"But, my dear sir," Mr. Thrall returned, "don't we *pay* for it? Do our servants object to rendering us this service?"

"That has nothing to do with the case; or, rather, it makes it worse. The fact that your servants do not object shows how completely they are depraved by usage. We should not object if they served you from affection, and if you repaid them in kindness; but the fact that you think you have made them a due return by giving them money shows how far from the right ideal in such a matter the whole capitalistic world is."

Here, to my great delight, Aristides spoke up:

"If the American practice were half as depraving as it ought logically to be in their conditions, their social system would drop to pieces. It was always astonishing to me that a people with their facilities for evil, their difficulties for good, should remain so kind and just and pure."

"That is what I understood from your letters to me, my dear Aristides. I am willing to leave the general argument for the present. But I should like to ask Mr. Thrall a question, and I hope it won't be offensive."

Mr. Thrall smiled. "At any rate I promise not to be offended."

" You are a very rich man?"

" Much richer than I would like to be."

" How rich?"

" Seventy millions; eighty; a hundred; three hundred; I don't just know."

" I don't suppose you've always felt your great wealth a great blessing?"

" A blessing? There have been times when I felt it a millstone hanged about my neck, and could have wished nothing so much as that I were thrown into the sea. Man, you don't *know* what a curse I have felt my money to be at such times. When I have given it away, as I have by millions at a time, I have never been sure that I was not doing more harm than good with it. I have hired men to seek out good objects for me, and I have tried my best to find for myself causes and institutions and persons who might be helped without hindering others as worthy, but sometimes it seems as if every dollar of my money carried a blight with it, and infected whoever touched it with a moral pestilence. It has reached a sum where the wildest profligate couldn't spend it, and it grows and grows. It's as if it were a rising flood that had touched my lips, and would go over my head before I could reach the shore. I believe I got it honestly, and I have tried to share it with those whose labor earned it for me. I have founded schools and hospitals and homes for old men and old women, and asylums for children, and the blind, and deaf, and dumb, and halt, and mad. Wherever I have found one of my old workmen in need, and I have looked personally into the matter, I have provided for him fully, short of pauperization. Where I have heard of some gifted youth, I have had him educated in the line of his gift. I have collected a gallery of works of art, and opened it on Sundays as well as week-days to the public free. If there is a story of famine, far or near, I send food by the ship-load. If there is any great public calamity, my agents have instructions to come to the rescue without refer-ring the case to me. But it is all useless! The money grows and grows, and I begin to feel that my efforts to employ it wisely and wholesomely are making me a public laughing-stock as well as an easy mark for every swindler with a job or a scheme." He turned abrupt-ly to me. "But you must often have heard the same from my old friend Strange. We used to talk these things over together, when our money was not the heap that mine is now; and it seems to me I can hear his voice saying the very words I have been using."

I, too, seemed to hear his voice in the words, and it was as if speaking from his grave.

I looked at Aristides, and read compassion in his dear face; but the face of Cyril remained severe and ju-dicial. He said: "Then, if what you say is true, you cannot think it a hardship if we remove your burden for the time you remain with us. I have consulted with the National and Regional as well as the Com-munal authorities, and we cannot let you continue to live in the manner you are living here. You must pay your way."

"I shall be only too glad to do that," Mr. Thrall returned, more cheerfully. "We have not a great deal of cash in hand, but I can give you my check on London or Paris or New York."

"In Altruria," Cyril returned, "we have no use for money. You must *pay* your way as soon as your pres-ent provision from your yacht is exhausted."

Mr. Thrall turned a dazed look on the young lord, who suggested: "I don't think we follow you. How can Mr. Thrall pay his way except with money?"

"He must pay with *work*. As soon as you come upon the neighbors here for the necessities of life you must all work. To-morrow or the next day or next week at the furthest you must go to work, or you must starve." Then he came out with that text of Scripture which had been so efficient with the crew of the *Little Sally:* "For even when we were with you this we commanded you, that if any would not work neither should he eat."

Lord Moors seemed very interested, and not so much surprised as I had expected. "Yes, I have often thought of that passage and of its susceptibility to a simpler interpretation than we usually give it. But—"

"There is but one interpretation of which it is susceptible," Cyril interrupted. "The apostle gives that interpretation when he prefaces the text with the words, 'For yourselves know how you ought to follow us; for we behaved not ourselves disorderly among you. Neither did we eat any man's bread for nought; but *wrought with travail* night and day, that we might not be chargeable to any of you: not because we have not power, but to make ourselves an ensample unto you to follow us.' The whole economy of Altruria is founded on these passages."

"Literally?"

"Literally."

"But, my dear sir," the young lord reasoned, "you surely do not wrench the text from some such meaning as that if a man has money, he may pay his way without working?"

"No, certainly not. But here you have no money, and as we cannot suffer any to 'walk among us disorderly, working not at all,' we must not exempt you from our rule."

XII

At this point there came a sound from within the marquee as of skirts sweeping forward sharply, imperiously, followed by a softer *frou-frou,* and Mrs. Thrall put aside the curtain of the tent with one hand, and stood challenging our little Altrurian group, while Lady Moors peered timidly at us from over her mother's shoulder. I felt a lust of battle rising in me at sight of that woman, and it was as much as I could do to control myself; but in view of the bad time I knew she was going to have, I managed to hold in, though I joined very scantly in the polite greetings of the Chrysostoms and Aristides, which she ignored as if they had been the salutations of savages. She glared at her husband for explanation, and he said, gently, " This is a delegation from the Altrurian capital, my dear, and we have been talking over the situation together."

" But what is this," she demanded, " that I have heard about our not paying? Do they accuse us of not paying? You could buy and sell the whole country."

I never imagined so much mildness could be put into such offensive words as Cyril managed to get into his answer. " We accuse you of not paying, and we do not mean that you shall become chargeable to us. The men and women who served you on shipboard have been put to work, and you must go to work, too."

" Mr. Thrall — Lord Moors — have you allowed these people to treat you as if you were part of the

206

ship's crew? Why don't you give them what they want and let them go? Of course it's some sort of blackmailing scheme. But you ought to get rid of them at any cost. Then you can appeal to the authorities, and tell them that you will bring the matter to the notice of the government at Washington. They must be taught that they cannot insult American citizens with impunity." No one spoke, and she added, " What do they really want?"

" Well, my dear," her husband hesitated, " I hardly know how to explain. But it seems that they think our living here in the way we do is disorderly, and— and they want us to go to work, in short."

" To *work!*" she shouted.

" Yes, all of us. That is, so I understand."

" What nonsense!"

She looked at us one after another, and when her eye rested on me, I began to suspect that insolent as she was she was even duller; in fact, that she was so sodden in her conceit of wealth that she was plain stupid. So when she said to me, " You are an American by birth, I believe. Can you tell me the meaning of this?" I answered:

" Cyril Chrysostom represents the authorities. If *he* asks me to speak, I will speak." Cyril nodded at me with a smile, and I went on. " It is a very simple matter. In Altruria everybody works with his hands three hours a day. After that he works or not, as he likes."

" What have we to do with that?" she asked.

" The rule has no exceptions."

" But we are not Altrurians; we are Americans."

" I am an American, too, and I work three hours every day, unless I am passing from one point to another on public business with my husband. Even then we prefer to stop during the work-hours, and help in the fields, or in the shops, or wherever we are needed. I left my own mother at home doing her kitchen work yesterday afternoon, though it was out of hours, and she need not have worked."

"Very well, then, we will do nothing of the kind, neither I, nor my daughter, nor my husband. He has worked hard all his life, and he has come away for a much-needed rest. I am not going to have him breaking himself down."

I could not help suggesting, "I suppose the men at work in his mines, and mills, and on his railroads and steamship lines are taking a much-needed rest, too. I hope you are not going to let them break themselves down, either."

Aristides gave me a pained glance, and Cyril and his wife looked grave, but she not quite so grave as he. Lord Moors said, "We don't seem to be getting on. What Mrs. Thrall fails to see, and I confess I don't quite see it myself, is that if we are not here *in forma pauperis*—"

"But you *are* here *in forma pauperis*," Cyril interposed, smilingly.

"How is that? If we are willing to pay—if Mr. Thrall's credit is undeniably good—"

"Mr. Thrall's credit is not good in Altruria; you can pay here only in one currency, in the sweat of your faces."

"You want us to be Tolstoys, I suppose," Mrs. Thrall said, contemptuously.

Cyril replied, gently, "The endeavor of Tolstoy, in capitalistic conditions, is necessarily dramatic. Your labor here will be for your daily bread, and it will be real." The inner dulness of the woman came into her eyes again, and he addressed himself to Lord Moors in continuing: "If a company of indigent people were cast away on an English coast, after you had rendered them the first aid, what should you do?"

The young man reflected. "I suppose we should put them in the way of earning a living until some ship arrived to take them home."

"That is merely what we propose to do in your case here," Cyril said.

"But we are not indigent—"

"Yes, you are absolutely destitute. You have money and credit, but neither has any value in Altruria. Nothing but work or love has any value in Altruria. You cannot realize too clearly that you stand before us *in forma pauperis*. But we require of you nothing that we do not require of ourselves. In Altruria every one is poor till he pays with work; then, for that time, he is rich; and he cannot otherwise lift himself above charity, which, except in the case of the helpless, we consider immoral. Your life here offers a very corrupting spectacle. You are manifestly living without work, and you are served by people whose hire you are not able to pay."

"My dear sir," Mr. Thrall said at this point, with a gentle smile, "I think they are willing to take the chances of being paid."

"We cannot suffer them to do so. At present we know of no means of your getting away from Altruria. We have disused our custom of annually connecting with the Australasian steamers, and it may be years before a vessel touches on our coast. A ship sailed for Boston some months ago, with the promise of returning in order that the crew may cast in their lot with us permanently. We do not confide in that promise, and you must therefore conform to our rule of life. Understand clearly that the willingness of your servants to serve you has nothing to do with the matter. That is part of the falsity in which the whole capitalistic world lives. As the matter stands with you, here, there is as much reason why you should serve them as they should serve you. If on their side they should elect to serve you from love, they will be allowed to do so. Otherwise, you and they must go to work with the neighbors at the tasks they will assign you."

"Do you mean at once?" Lord Moors asked.

"The hours of the obligatory labors are nearly past for the day. But if you are interested in learning what you will be set to doing to-morrow, the Communal authorities will be pleased to instruct you during the Voluntaries this afternoon. You may be sure that in no case will your weakness or inexperience be overtasked. Your histories will be studied, and appropriate work will be assigned to each of you."

Mrs. Thrall burst out, "If you think I am going into my kitchen—"

Then I burst in, "I left my mother in *her* kitchen!"

"And a very fit place for her, I dare say," she retorted, but Lady Moors caught her mother's arm and murmured, in much the same distress as showed in my husband's mild eyes, "Mother! Mother!" and drew her within.

XIII

WELL, Dolly, I suppose you will think it was pretty hard for those people, and when I got over my temper I confess that I felt sorry for the two men, and for the young girl whom the Altrurians would not call Lady Moors, but addressed by her Christian name, as they did each of the American party in his or her turn; even Mrs. Thrall had to answer to Rebecca. They were all rather bewildered, and so were the butler and the footmen, and the *chef* and his helpers, and the ladies' maids. These were even more shocked than those they considered their betters, and I quite took to my affections Lord Moors' man Robert, who was in an awe-stricken way trying to get some light from me on the situation. He contributed as much as any one to bring about a peaceful submission to the inevitable, for he had been a near witness of what had happened to the crew when they attempted their rebellion to the authorities; but he did not profess to understand the matter, and from time to time he seemed to question the reality of it.

The two masters, as you would call Mr. Thrall and Lord Moors, both took an attitude of amiable curiosity towards their fate, and accepted it with interest when they had partly chosen and partly been chosen by it. Mr. Thrall had been brought up on a farm till his ambition carried him into the world; and he found the light gardening assigned him for his first task by no means a hardship. He was rather critical of the

Altrurian style of hoe at first, but after he got the hang of it, as he said, he liked it better, and during the three hours of the first morning's Obligatories, his ardor to cut all the weeds out at once had to be restrained rather than prompted. He could not be persuaded to take five minutes for rest out of every twenty, and he could not get over his life-long habit of working against time. The Altrurians tried to make him understand that here people must not work *against* time, but must always work *with* it, so as to have enough work to do each day; otherwise they must remain idle during the Obligatories and tend to demoralize the workers. It seemed that Lady Moors had a passion for gardening, and she was set to work with her father on the border of flowers surrounding the vegetable patch he was hoeing. She knew about flowers, and from her childhood had amused herself by growing them, and so far from thinking it a hardship or disgrace to dig, she was delighted to get at them. It was easy to see that she and her father were cronies, and when I went round in the morning with Aristides to ask if we could do anything for them, we heard them laughing and talking gayly together before we reached them. They said they had looked their job (as Mr. Thrall called it) over the afternoon before during the Voluntaries, and had decided how they would manage, and they had set to work that morning as soon as they had breakfast. Lady Moors had helped her mother get the breakfast, and she seemed to regard the whole affair as a picnic, though from the look of Mrs. Thrall's back, as she turned it on me, when I saw her coming to the door of the marquee with a coffee-pot in her hand, I decided that she was not yet resigned to her new lot in life.

Lord Moors was nowhere to be seen, and I felt some

little curiosity about him which was not quite anxiety.
Later, as we were going back to our quarters in the
village, we saw him working on the road with a party
of Altrurians who were repairing a washout from an
overnight rain. They were having all kinds of a
time, except a bad time, trying to understand each
other in their want of a common language. It appeared that the Altrurians were impressed with his
knowledge of road-making, and were doing something
which he had indicated to them by signs. We offered
our services as interpreters, and then he modestly
owned in defence of his suggestions that when he was
at Oxford he had been one of the band of enthusiastic
undergraduates who had built a piece of highway
under Mr. Ruskin's direction. The Altrurians regarded his suggestions as rather amateurish, but they
were glad to act upon them, when they could, out of
pure good feeling and liking for him; and from time
to time they rushed upon him and shook hands with
him; their affection did not go further, and he was
able to stand the handshaking, though he told us he
hoped they would not feel it necessary to keep it up,
for it was really only a very simple matter like putting a culvert in place of a sluice which they had been
using to carry the water off. They understood what
he was saying, from his gestures, and they crowded
round us to ask whether he would like to join them
during the Voluntaries that afternoon, in getting the
stone out of a neighboring quarry, and putting in the
culvert at once. We explained to him, and he said
he should be very happy. All the time he was looking at them admirably, and he said, " It's really very
good," and we understood that he meant their classic
working-dress, and when he added, " I should really
fancy trying it myself one day," and we told them,

they wanted to go and bring him an Altrurian costume at once. But we persuaded them not to urge him, and in fact he looked very fit for his work in his yachting flannels.

I talked him over a long time with Aristides, and tried to get his point of view. I decided finally that an Englishman of his ancient lineage and high breeding, having voluntarily come down to the level of an American millionaire by marriage, could not feel that he was lowering himself any further by working with his hands. In fact, he probably felt that his merely undertaking a thing dignified the thing; but of course this was only speculation on my part, and he may have been resigned to working for a living because like poor people elsewhere he was obliged to do it. Aristides thought there was a good deal in that idea, but it is hard for an Altrurian to conceive of being ashamed of work, for they regard idleness as pauperism, and they would look upon our leisure classes, so far as we have them, very much as we look upon tramps, only they would make the excuse for our tramps that they often cannot get work.

We had far more trouble with the servants than we had with the masters in making them understand that they were to go to work in the fields and shops, quite as the crew of the yacht had done. Some of them refused outright, and stuck to their refusal until the village electrician rescued them with the sort of net and electric filament which had been employed with the recalcitrant sailors; others were brought to a better mind by withholding food from them till they were willing to pay for it by working. You will be sorry to learn, Dolly, that the worst of the rebels were the ladies' maids, who, for the honor of our sex, ought not to have required the application of the net and filament; but they had not such appetites as the men-servants, and did not mind starving so much. However, in a very short time they were at work, too, and more or less resigned, though they did not profess to understand it.

You will think me rather fickle, I am afraid, but after I made the personal acquaintance of Mr. Thrall's *chef,* Anatole, I found my affections dividing themselves between him and his lordship's man Robert, my first love. But Anatole was magnificent, a gaunt, little, aquiline man, with a branching mustache and gallant goatee, and having held an exalted position at a salary of ten thousand a year from Mr. Thrall, he could easily stoop from it, while poor Robert was tormented with misgivings, not for himself, but for Lord and Lady Moors and Mr. Thrall. It became my pleasing office to explain the situation to Monsieur Anatole, who, when he imagined it, gave a cry of joy, and confessed, what he had never liked to tell Mr. Thrall, knowing the misconceptions of Americans on the subject, that he had belonged in France to a party of which the political and social ideal was almost identical with that of the Altrurians. He asked for an early opportunity of addressing the village Assembly and explaining this delightful circumstance in public, and he profited by the occasion to embrace the first Altrurian we met and kiss him on both cheeks.

His victim was a messenger from the Commune, who had been sent to inquire whether Anatole had a preference as to the employment which should be assigned to him, and I had to reply for him that he was a man of science; that he would be happy to serve the republic in whatever capacity his concitizens chose, but that he thought he could be most useful in studying the comestible vegetation of the neighborhood, and the substitution of the more succulent herbs for the flesh-meats to the use of which, he understood from me, the Altrurians were opposed. In the course of his preparation for the rôle of *chef,* which he had played both in France and America, he had made a specialty of edible fungi; and the result was that Anatole was set to mushrooming, and up to this moment he has discovered no less than six species hitherto unknown to the Altrurian table. This has added to their dietary in several important particulars, the fungi he has discovered being among those highly decorative and extremely poisonous - looking sorts which flourish in the deep woods and offer themselves almost inexhaustibly in places near the ruins of the old capitalistic cities, where hardly any other foods will grow. Anatole is very proud of his success, and at more than one Communal Assembly has lectured upon his discoveries and treated of their preparation for the table, with sketches of them as he found them growing, colored after nature by his own hand. He has himself become a fanatical vegetarian, having, he confesses, always had a secret loathing for the meats he stooped to direct the cooking of among the French and American bourgeoisie in the days which he already looks back upon as among the most benighted of his history.

XIV

THE scene has changed again, Dolly, and six months have elapsed without your knowing it. Aristides and I long ago completed the tour of the capitals which the Thrall incident interrupted, and we have been settled for many months in the Maritime Capital, where it has been decided we had better fill out the first two years of my husband's repatriation. I have become more and more thoroughly naturalized, and if I am not yet a perfect Altrurian, it is not for not loving better and better the best Altrurian of them all, and not for not admiring and revering this wonderful civilization.

During the Obligatories of the forenoons I do my housework with my own hands, and as my mother lives with us we have long talks together, and try to make each other believe that the American conditions were a sort of nightmare from which we have happily awakened. You see how terribly frank I am, my dear, but if I were not, I could not make you understand how I feel. My heart aches for you, there, and the more because I know that you do not want to live differently, that you are proud of your economic and social illogicality, and that you think America is the best country under the sun! I can never persuade you, but if you could only come here, once, and see for yourselves! Seeing would be believing, and believing would be the wish never to go away, but to be at home here always.

I can imagine your laughing at me and asking Mr.

Makely whether the *Little Sally* has ever returned to Altruria, and how I can account for the captain's failure to keep his word. I confess that is a sore point with me. It is now more than a year since she sailed, and, of course, we have not had a sign or whisper from her. I could almost wish that the crew were willing to stay away, but I am afraid it is the captain who is keeping them. It has become almost a mania with me, and every morning, the first thing when I wake, I go for my before-breakfast walk along the marble terrace that overlooks the sea, and scan the empty rounding for the recreant ship. I do not want to think so badly of human nature, as I must if the *Little Sally* never comes back, and I am sure you will not blame me if I should like her to bring me some word from you. I know that if she ever reached Boston you got my letters and presents, and that you have been writing me as faithfully as I have been writing you, and what a sheaf of letters from you there will be if her masts ever pierce the horizon! To tell the truth, I do long for a little American news! Do you still keep on murdering and divorcing, and drowning, and burning, and mommicking, and maiming people by sea and land? Has there been any war since I left? Is the financial panic as great as ever, and is there as much hunger and cold? I know that whatever your crimes and calamities are, your heroism and martyrdom, your wild generosity and self-devotion, are equal to them.

It is no use to pretend that in little over a year I can have become accustomed to the eventlessness of life in Altruria. I go on for a good many days together and do not miss the exciting incidents you have in America, and then suddenly I am wolfishly hungry for the old sensations, just as now and then I *want meat,* though I know I should loathe the sight and smell of it if I came within reach of it. You would laugh, I dare say, at the Altrurian papers, and what they print for news. Most of the space is taken up with poetry, and character study in the form of fiction, and scientific inquiry of every kind. But now and then there is a report of the production of a new play in one of the capitals; or an account of an open - air pastoral in one of the communes; or the progress of some public work, like the extension of the National Colonnade; or the wonderful liberation of some section from malaria; or the story of some good man or woman's life, ended at the patriarchal age they reach here. They also print selected passages of capitalistic history, from the earliest to the latest times, showing how in war and pestilence and needless disaster the world outside Altruria remains essentially the same that it was at the beginning of civilization, with some slight changes through the changes of human nature for the better in its slow approaches to the Altrurian ideal. In noting these changes the writers get some sad amusement out of the fact that the capitalistic world believes human nature cannot be changed, though cannibalism and slavery and polygamy have all been extirpated in the so-called Christian countries, and these things were once human nature, which is always changing, while brute nature remains the same. Now and then they touch very guardedly on that slavery, worse than war, worse than any sin or shame conceivable to the Altrurians, in which uncounted myriads of women are held and bought and sold, and they have to note that in this the capitalistic world is without the hope of better things. You know what I mean, Dolly; every good woman knows the little she cannot help knowing; but if you had ever inquired into that horror, as I once felt obliged to do, you would think it the blackest hor-

219

ror of the state of things where it must always exist as long as there are riches and poverty. Now, when so many things in America seem bad dreams, I cannot take refuge in thinking that a bad dream; the reality was so deeply burnt into my brain by the words of some of the slaves; and when I think of it I want to grovel on the ground with my mouth in the dust. But I know this can only distress you, for you cannot get away from the fact as I have got away from it; that there it is in the next street, perhaps in the next house, and that any night when you leave your home with your husband, you may meet it at the first step from your door.

You can very well imagine what a godsend the reports of Aristides and the discussions of them have been to our papers. They were always taken down stenographically, and they were printed like dialogue, so that at a little distance you would take them at first for murder trials or divorce cases, but when you look closer, you find them questions and answers about the state of things in America. There are often humorous passages, for the Altrurians are inextinguishably amused by our illogicality, and what they call the perpetual *non sequiturs* of our lives and laws. In the discussions they frequently burlesque these, but as they present them they seem really beyond the wildest burlesque. Perhaps you will be surprised to know that a nation of working-people like these feel more compassion than admiration for our working-people. They pity them, but they blame them more than they blame the idle rich for the existing condition of things in America. They ask why, if the American workmen are in the immense majority, they do not vote a true and just state, and why they go on striking and starving their families instead; they cannot distinguish in principle between the confederations of labor and the combinations of capital, between the trusts and the trades-unions, and they condemn even more severely the oppressions and abuses of the unions. My husband tries to explain that the unions are merely provisional, and are a temporary means of enabling the employees to stand up against the tyranny of the employers, but they always come back and ask him if the workmen have not most of the votes, and if they have, why they do not protect themselves peacefully instead of organizing themselves in fighting shape, and making a warfare of industry.

There is not often anything so much like news in the Altrurian papers as the grounding of the Thrall yacht on the coast of the Seventh Region, and the incident has been treated and discussed in every possible phase by the editors and their correspondents. They have been very frank about it, as they are about everything in Altruria, and they have not concealed their anxieties about their unwelcome guests. They got on without much trouble in the case of the few sailors of the *Lillle Bully,* but the crew of the *Saraband* is so large that it is a different matter. In the first place, they do not like the application of force, even in the mild electrical form in which they employ it, and they fear that the effect with themselves will be bad, however good it is for their guests. Besides, they dread the influence which a number of people, invested with the charm of strangeness, may have with the young men and especially the young girls of the neighborhood. The hardest thing the Altrurians have to grapple with is feminine curiosity, and the play of this about the strangers is what they seek the most anxiously to control. Of course, you will think it funny, and I must say that it seemed so to me at first, but I have come

to think it is serious. The Altrurian girls are cultivated and refined, but as they have worked all their
lives with their hands they cannot imagine the difference that work makes in Americans; that it coarsens
and classes them, especially if they have been in immediate contact with rich people, and been degraded or
brutalized by the knowledge of the contempt in which
labor is held among us by those who are not compelled
to it. Some of my Altrurian friends have talked it
over with me, and I could take their point of view,
though secretly I could not keep my poor American
feelings from being hurt when they said that to have a
large number of people from the capitalistic world
thrown upon their hands was very much as it would
be with us if we had the same number of Indians, with
all their tribal customs and ideals, thrown upon our
hands. They say they will not shirk their duty in the
matter, and will study it carefully; but all the same,
they wish the incident had not happened.

XV

I AM glad that I was called away from the disagreeable point I left in my last, and that I have got back temporarily to the scene of the Altrurianization of Mr. Thrall and his family. So far as it has gone it is perfect, if I may speak from the witness of happiness in those concerned, except perhaps Mrs. Thrall; she is as yet only partially reconstructed, but even she has moments of forgetting her lost grandeur and of really enjoying herself in her work. She is an excellent housekeeper, and she has become so much interested in making the marquee a simple home for her family that she is rather proud of showing it off as the effect of her unaided efforts. She was allowed to cater to them from the canned meats brought ashore from the yacht as long as they would stand it, but the wholesome open-air conditions have worked a wonderful change in them, and neither Mr. Thrall nor Lord and Lady Moors now have any taste for such dishes. Here Mrs. Thrall's old-time skill as an excellent vegetable cook, when she was the wife of a young mechanic, has come into play, and she believes that she sets the best table in the whole neighborhood, with fruits and many sorts of succulents and the everlasting and ever-pervading mushrooms.

As the Altrurians do not wish to annoy their involuntary guests, or to interfere with their way of life where they do not consider it immoral, their control has ended with setting them to work for a living. They have not asked them to the communal refectory, but, as long as they have been content to serve each other, have allowed them their private table. Of course, their adaptation to their new way of life has proceeded more slowly than it otherwise would, but with the exception of Mrs. Thrall they are very intelligent people, and I have been charmed in talking the situation over with them. The trouble has not been so great with the ship's people, as was feared. Such of these as have imagined their stay here permanent, or wished it to be so, have been received into the neighboring communes, and have taken the first steps towards naturalization; those who look forward to getting away some time, or express the wish for it, are allowed to live in a community of their own, where they are not molested as long as they work in the three hours of the Obligatories. Naturally, they are kept out of mischief, but after their first instruction in the ideas of public property and the impossibility of enriching themselves at the expense of any one else, they have behaved very well. The greatest trouble they ever gave was in trapping and killing the wild things for food; but when they were told that this must not be done, and taught to recognize the vast range of edible fungi, they took not unwillingly to mushrooms and the ranker tubers and roots, from which, with unlimited eggs, cheese, milk, and shell-fish, they have constructed a diet of which they do not complain.

This brings me rather tangentially to Monsieur Anatole, who has become a fanatical Altrurian, and has even had to be restrained in some of his enthusiastic plans for the compulsory naturalization of his fellow castaways. His value as a scientist has been cordially recognized, and his gifts as an artist in the exquisite water-color studies of edible fungi has won his notice in the capital of the Seventh Regional where they have been shown at the spring water-color exhibition. He has printed several poems in the *Regional Gazette,* villanelles, rondeaux, and triolets, with accompanying versions of the French, into Altrurian by one of the first Altrurian poets. This is a widow of about Monsieur Anatole's own age; and the literary friendship between them has ripened into something much more serious. In fact they are engaged to be married. I suppose you will laugh at this, Dolly, and at first I confess that there was enough of the old American in me to be shocked at the idea of a French *chef* marrying an Altrurian lady who could trace her descent to the first Altrurian president of the Commonwealth, and who is universally loved and honored. I could not help letting something of the kind escape me by accident, to a friend, and presently Mrs. Chrysostom was sent to interview me on the subject, and to learn just how the case appeared to me. This put me on my honor, and I was obliged to say how it would appear in America, though every moment I grew more and more ashamed of myself and my native country, where we pretend that labor is honorable, and are always heaping dishonor on it. I told how certain of our girls and matrons had married their coachmen and riding-masters and put themselves at odds with society, and I confessed that marrying a cook would be regarded as worse, if possible.

Mrs. Chrysostom was accompanied by a lady in her second youth, very graceful, very charmingly dressed, and with an expression of winning intelligence, whom she named to me simply as Cecilia, in the Altrurian fashion. She apparently knew no English, and at first Mrs. Chrysostom translated each of her questions and my answers. When I had got through, this lady began to question me herself in Altrurian, which I owned to understanding a little. She said:

" You know Anatole ?"

" Yes, certainly, and I like him, as I think every one must who knows him."

" He is a skilful *chef?*"

" Mr. Thrall would not have paid him ten thousand dollars a year if he had not been."

" You have seen some of his water-colors ?"

" Yes. They are exquisite. He is unquestionably an artist of rare talent."

" And it is known to you that he is a man of scientific attainments ?"

" That is something I cannot judge of so well as Aristides; but *he* says M. Anatole is learned beyond any man he knows in edible fungi."

" As an adoptive Altrurian, and knowing the American ideas from our point of view, should you respect their ideas of social inequality ?"

" Not the least in the world. I understand as well as you do that their ideas must prevail wherever one works for a living and another does not. Those ideas are practically as much accepted in America as they are in Europe, but I have fully renounced them."

You see, Dolly, how far I have gone!

The unknown, who could be pretty easily imagined, rose up and gave me her hand. " If you are in the Region on the third of May you must come to our wedding."

The same afternoon I had a long talk with Mr. Thrall, whom I found at work replanting a strawberry-patch during the Voluntaries. He rose up at the sound of my voice, and after an old man's dim moment for getting me mentally in focus, he brightened into a genial smile, and said, " Oh, Mrs. Homos! I am glad to see you."

I told him to go on with his planting, and I offered to get down on my knees beside him and help, but he gallantly handed me to a seat in the shade beside his daughter's flower-bed, and it was there that we had a long talk about conditions in 'America and Altruria, and how he felt about the great change in his life.

" Well, I can truly say," he answered much more at length than I shall report, " that I have never been so happy since the first days of my boyhood. All care has dropped from me; I don't feel myself rich, and I don't feel myself poor in this perfect safety from want. The only thing that gives me any regret is that my present state has not been the effect of my own will and deed. If I am now following the greatest and truest of all counsels it has not been because I have sold all and given to the poor, but because my money has been mercifully taken from me, and I have been released from its responsibilities in a state of things where there is no money."

" But, Mr. Thrall," I said, " don't you ever feel that you have a duty to the immense fortune which you have left in 'America, and which must be disposed of somehow when people are satisfied that you are not going to return and dispose of it yourself ?"

" No, none. I was long ago satisfied that I could really do no good with it. Perhaps if I had had more faith in it I might have done some good with it, but I believe that I never did anything but harm, even when I seemed to be helping the most, for I was aiding in the perpetuation of a state of things essentially wrong. Now, if I never go back—and I never wish to go back—let the law dispose of it as seems best to the authorities. I have no kith or kin, and my wife has none, so there is no one to feel aggrieved by its application to public objects."

" And how do you imagine it will be disposed of ?"

" Oh, I suppose for charitable and educational purposes. Of course a good deal of it will go in graft; but that cannot be helped."

" But if you could now dispose of it according to your clearest ideas of justice, and if you were forced to make the disposition yourself, what would you do with it ?"

" Well, that is something I have been thinking of, and as nearly as I can make out, I ought to go into the records of my prosperity and ascertain just how and when I made my money. Then I ought to seek out as fully as possible the workmen who helped me make it by their labor. Their wages, which were always the highest, were never a fair share, though I forced myself to think differently, and it should be my duty to inquire for them and pay them each a fair share, or, if they are dead, then their children or their next of kin. But even when I had done this I should not be sure that I had not done them more harm than good."

How often I had heard poor Mr. Strange say things like this, and heard of other rich men saying them, after lives of what is called beneficence! Mr. Thrall drew a deep sigh, and cast a longing look at his strawberry-bed. I laughed, and said, " You are anxious to get back to your plants, and I won't keep you. I wonder if Mrs. Thrall could see me if I called; or Lady Moors ?"

He said he was sure they would, and I took my way over to the marquee. I was a little surprised to be met at the door by Lord Moors' man Robert. He told me he was very sorry, but her ladyship was helping his lordship at a little job on the roads, which they were doing quite in the Voluntaries, with the hope of having the National Colonnade extended to a given point; the ladies were helping the gentlemen get the place in shape. He was still sorrier, but I not so much, that Mrs. Thrall was lying down and would like to be excused; she was rather tired from putting away the luncheon things.

He asked me if I would not sit down, and he offered me one of the camp-stools at the door of the marquee, and I did sit down for a moment, while he flitted about the interior doing various little things. At last I said, "How is this, Robert? I thought you had been assigned to a place in the communal refectory. You're not here on the old terms?"

He came out and stood respectfully holding a dusting - cloth in his hand. "Thank you, not exactly, ma'am. But the fact is, ma'am, that the communal monitors have allowed me to come back here a few hours in the afternoon, on what I may call terms of my own."

"I don't understand. But won't you sit down, Robert?"

"Thank you, if it is the same to you, ma'am, I would rather stand while I'm here. In the refectory, of course, it's different."

"But about your own terms?"

"Thanks. You see, ma'am, I've thought all along it was a bit awkward for them here, they not being so much used to looking after things, and I asked leave to come and help now and then. Of course, they said that I could not be allowed to serve for hire in Altruria; and one thing led to another, and I said it would really be a favor to me, and I didn't expect money for my work, for I did not suppose I should ever be where I

229

could use it again, but if they would let me come here and do it for—"

Robert stopped and blushed and looked down, and I took the word, " For love ?"

" Well, ma'am, that's what they called it."

Dolly, it made the tears come into my eyes, and I said very solemnly, " Robert, do you know, I believe you are the sweetest soul even in this land flowing with milk and honey ?"

" Oh, you mustn't say that, ma'am. There's Mr. Thrall and his lordship and her ladyship. I'm sure they would do the like for me if I needed their help. And there are the Altrurians, you know."

" But they are used to it, Robert, and—Robert! Be frank with me! What do you think of Altruria ?"

" Quite frank, ma'am, as if you were not connected with it, as you are ?"

" Quite frank."

" Well, ma'am, if you are sure you wouldn't mind it, or consider it out of the way for me, I should say it was—rum."

" *Rum?* Don't you think it is beautiful here, to see people living *for* each other instead of living *on* each other, and the whole nation like one family, and the country a paradise ?"

" Well, that's just it, ma'am, if you won't mind my saying so. That's what I mean by rum."

" Won't you explain ?"

" It doesn't seem *real*. Every night when I go to sleep, and think that there isn't a thief or a policeman on the whole continent, and only a few harmless homicides, as you call them, that wouldn't hurt a fly, and not a person hungry or cold, and no poor and no rich, and no servants and no masters, and no soldiers, and no —disreputable characters, it seems as if I was going to

230

wake up in the morning and find myself on the *Saraband* and it all a dream here."

"Yes, Robert," I had to own, "that was the way with me, too, for a long while. And even now I have dreams about America and the way matters are there, and I wake myself weeping for fear Altruria *isn't* true. Robert! You must be honest with me! When you are awake, and it's broad day, and you see how happy every one is here, either working or playing, and the whole land without an ugly place in it, and the lovely villages and the magnificent towns, and everything, does it still seem—rum?"

"It's like that, ma'am, at times. I don't say at all times."

"And you don't believe that the rest of the world — England and America — will ever be rum, too?"

"I don't see how they can. You see the poor are against it as well as the rich. Everybody wants to have something of his own, and the trouble seems to come from that. I don't suppose it was brought about in a day, Altruria wasn't, ma'am?"

"No, it was whole centuries coming."

"That was what I understood from that Mr. Chrysostom—Cyril, he wants me to call him, but I can't quite make up my mouth to it—who speaks English, and says he has been in England. He was telling me about it, one day when we were drying the dishes at the refectory together. He says they used to have wars and trusts and trades-unions here in the old days, just as we do now in civilized countries."

"And you don't consider Altruria civilized?"

"Well, not in just that sense of the word, ma'am. You wouldn't call heaven civilized?"

"Well, not in just that sense of the word, Robert."

231

"You see, it's rum here, because, though everything seems to go so right, it's against human nature."

"The Altrurians say it isn't."

"I hope I don't differ from you, ma'am, but what would people—the best people—at home say? They would say it wasn't reasonable; they would say it wasn't even possible. That's what makes me think it's a dream—that it's rum. Begging your pardon, ma'am."

"Oh, I quite understand, Robert. Then you don't believe a camel can ever go through the eye of a needle?"

"I don't quite see how, ma'am."

"But you are proof of as great a miracle, Robert."

"Beg your pardon, ma'am?"

"Some day I will explain. But is there nothing that can make you believe Altruria is true here, and that it can be true anywhere?"

"I have been thinking a good deal about that, ma'am. One doesn't quite like to go about in a dream, or think one is dreaming, and I have got to saying to myself that if some ship was to come here from England or America, or even from Germany, and we could compare our feelings with the feelings of people who were fresh to it, we might somehow get to believe that it was real."

"Yes," I had to own. "We need fresh proofs from time to time. There was a ship that sailed from here something over a year ago, and the captain promised his crew to let them bring her back, but at times I am afraid that was part of the dream, too, and that we're all something I am dreaming about."

"Just so, ma'am," Robert said, and I came away downhearted enough, though he called after me, "Mrs. Thrall will be very sorry, ma'am."

Back in the Maritime Capital, and oh, Dolly, Dolly, Dolly! They have sighted the *Little Sally* from the terrace! How happy I am! There will be letters from you, and I shall hear all that has happened in America, and I shall never again doubt that Altruria is real! I don't know how I shall get these letters of mine back to you, but somehow it can be managed. Perhaps the *Saraband's* crew will like to take the *Little Sally* home again; perhaps when Mr. Thrall knows the ship is here he will want to buy it and go back to his money in America and the misery of it! Do you believe he will? Should I like to remind my husband of his promise to take me home on a visit? Oh, my heart misgives me! I wonder if the captain of the *Little Sally* has brought his wife and children with him, and is going to settle among us, or whether he has just let his men have the vessel, and they have come to Altruria without him? I dare not ask anything, I dare not think anything!

THE END